THE JAMES EDWARDS STORY

(From the Archives of a Digger's Son)

JOHN WELDON EVANS

DEDICATION

To the Silver Towns, the Silver People,

and

a Time and Place and a Love long gone

but Not Forgotten

Table of Contents

Introduction

The James Edwards Story is about the life and times of a second-generation Panamanian West Indian born and raised in the town of La Boca, C. Z. in the era when the United States occupied the Panama Canal Zone and operated the Panama Canal.

La Boca was one of many "silver" towns within the Canal Zone that were built by the U.S. to house non-U.S. construction workers and their families who were brought from the Caribbean islands in the late 1800's and early 1900's to dig the Panama Canal and help maintain its operation for six or more decades. While giving a lifetime of blood, sweat and tears to fulfill America's grand inter-oceanic dream, West Indian men and women, grossly underpaid, denied equal benefits and privileges, racially abused and segregated, lived in the Canal Zone "silver" towns and raised three generations there, not without sacrifices. Yet, with humility and faith, they endured. What was their reward?

It came to pass that all those "silver" towns, those once familiar sites to many, do not exist anymore. All are demolished or abandoned -- the homes vanquished, the workers all passed away and their descendants are all gone. What is left of those once familiar towns, if not carted away, or destroyed, is now the property of the Republic of Panama, as a result mainly of the Carter-Torrijos Treaty of 1977.

Today, the world does not remember, nor does it care about the people who had once lived, toiled, suffered, prayed, and strived together, with common fears and hopes and dreams, in those "silver" towns that are forgotten like forgotten debts and deeds. Yet, the world still profits from, still celebrates with great pride and great acclaim that Eighth Wonder of the Modern World, and thousands and thousands of ships and goods still sail through that stubborn ditch where many lives were crushed and bled. What were the rewards for those forgotten people, who once lived in Canal Zone "silver" towns and helped to build that marvelous wonder? And who remembers them? Somebody should remember them. And so, I'd like to tell you now about the James Edwards story.

This entire narrative is written in the third person and is based on the author's life which he portrays in the book under the name of James Edwards. Through this character the author reveals highlights of his birth, early childhood, adolescence, youth and adulthood. The story begins in La Boca, the author's birthplace, where it flourishes for awhile, then moves to the towns of Silver City and Colon, and finally arrives, like the stories of countless other West

Indians from similar Canal Zone "silver" towns, to the shores of the U. S. where a large community of expatriates from Panama and the Canal Zone resettled, after the handwriting written on the wall had predicted the end of U. S. occupation in the Panama Canal Zone.

The following are fictitious names used to represent real persons in the book, and any resemblance to people's names is coincidental:

Daryl Anders	Bertrand Martin
Pearlina Anders	William Mathewson
Rudolph Barnes	Agnes Peterson
Lisa Peterson	Samuel Peterson
Theresa Bingham	Delores Peterson
Francis Bingham	Naomi Peterson
Daisy Biggett	Sephora Reid
Beatrice Corbin	Rufus Reid, Sr.
Carlton Corbin, Sr.	Iona Reid
Lucas Corbin	Ilene Reid
Carlton Corbin, Jr.	Rufus Reid, Jr.
Marlene Corbin	Melia Reid
Harvey Corbin	Ronald Wilson
Lon Carswell	William Weakley
Richard Edwards	Marie Edwards
James Edwards	Ivy Edwards
Jean Edwards	Charles Edward

Chapter I:

The Early Years

The registry in the maternity ward of Gorgas Hospital, Ancon, Canal Zone, showed at exactly 8:38 a.m. on the morning of Tuesday, May 15, 1928, that Dr. G. M. Stevenson delivered a boy baby to Richard and Marie Edwards, proud parents who resided in the town of La Boca, C. Z. This was the last of seven children birthed to Mrs. Edwards (and as wise old people used to say: "He was her wash belly because he took everything that she had left, therefore he was a blessed child"). They christened him "James Baptist Edwards" in the St. Theresa Catholic Church in the town of La Boca, C.Z., where he grew up.

Being the last child in the family, he soon discovered, has its advantages. No more babies are coming after you and all who came before you have only you on whom to shower their love and kisses. What a blessing indeed! Everyone makes a fuss over you, wants to play with you and protect you if you are ever in harm's way. He also learned very early on the value and use of a good pair of lungs and a good "cry" (the louder the better) that always gets prompt attention as it did that afternoon in 1931 when he was three years old and his two sisters Ivy, 11, and Jean, 9, were pushing him in a little cart on the sidewalk on Guadeloupe Street in front of the St. Theresa Church. Suddenly a man they called "Braka" who lived in the street level apartment of the church building on Guadeloupe Street (It was said that he was the caretaker of the church) took exception to children playing outside and he burst out of the apartment fuming and cussing: "A man can't get no damn sleep around here; you children get to hell away from here..." and he accidentally knocked the cart almost turning it over on the sidewalk thereby committing a grievous offense. Little James went to work then and with all the power in the seemingly inexhaustible and vigorous vocal cords that God gave him, he made the loudest protest you could ever imagine until the whole neighborhood was aroused by the ear-shattering sound that brought his raging mother out from nowhere when she heard her baby screaming, and she pounced on that cringing, penitent neighbor who begged for mercy before she finished beating him to a pulp with a broomstick: "Take that... and that... you monster you... ah goin' kill you before I let you hurt my baby..." O what fury there is in a mother's wrath!

In the early days in La Boca after they had bulldozed and leveled the terrain, transplanted or built the first houses, paved new streets and sidewalks, they soon decided to put back some of nature's flora to restore the natural balance and improve the ecology, so they planted trees on many blocks, coconut palm trees, mango trees, breadfruit trees, golden apple trees, etc. The coconut palm trees were planted along a street running north and south through the center of the town called Jamaica Prado, and between the houses on many street corners they planted mango trees and other tropical trees. James was only four years old when La Boca was still a young community and these new plants needed nurturing and sustaining. So, every day in the dry season, and later less frequently, a horse-driven water truck would come by in the street watering the new plants so they would grow quickly. As the horse-driven water truck came up the street and went from block to block the clickety clackety of the horses' hoofs against the pavement made a rhythmic sound and in no time children (many of whom like James had never seen a live horse up close before) found it an entertaining experience to walk alongside the truck as it moved along and they made up words to go with the rhythm: "Hocus Pocus come from Bocas... (clickety clackety... clickety clackety...) Hocus Pocus come from Bocas... (clickety clackety... clickety clackety...).” Of course, James could only go near the horses when they passed by his block because at his age his parents didn’t allow him to roam too far from where he lived.

When he was 4-and-a-half years old he was curious about a lot of things, but he was especially attracted to the musical sounds made by the scissors grinder man on his flute whenever he passed through the streets of La Boca. James loved to hear those eight musical notes (one octave above middle “C”): *mi sol do mi, do mi sol do* coming from far off in the distance. When his mother heard them, she, too, was excited and she called out to her next-door neighbors: “The scissors grinder is here! ... The scissors grinder is here! ...” and James would run downstairs behind her so he wouldn’t miss the show for anything! The scissors grinder man would park his contraption in the yard and all the anxious housewives would gather around him. With his right foot busy pumping a spindle that swiftly turned a circular grindstone that dipped into water as it spun, and, with his hands guiding the blades with care as he pressed the steel blades against the grindstone and brilliant sparks flew out into the air like fireworks, the scissors grinder man would sharpen all the neighbors’ knives, scissors, and cutleries until the edges were extremely sharp and he would test each with his fingertips and his keen eye then he would give the customer a wink and a nod meaning that the job was done to his satisfaction and the cutleries were ready to perform again their miracles in the housewives' kitchens and on seamstresses' sewing boards. When the last pair of scissors and the last blade was sharpened, he mounted onto the front of his contraption and pedaled away down the street, and you could hear him blowing his flute in the distance as he disappeared: mi sol do mi... do mi sol do.

When James was five, since they did not have any kindergarten classes yet, his mother placed him with Mrs. St. Hilaire who ran a pre-school that she taught under the cellar of house 1018. In the early days in La Boca there were several dame schools run by women who came from the islands with some primary school teaching experience (like Mrs. Vassal, Mrs. Rance, Mrs. Mulcare, Mrs. St. Hilaire, etc.) and some taught out of British reading texts like the British Royal Readers, etc. They taught the three R's (reading, 'riting, 'rithmetic mostly by rote followed by recitation). In time, these dame schools went out of fashion when the modern La Boca elementary and junior high school was built.

On July 9, 1934, when James was six years old, his mother enrolled him into the La Boca Elementary School built on the banks overlooking the Pacific

Ocean near the mouth of the Panama Canal. During that same week, on Thursday, July 12, 1934, Franklin Delano Roosevelt, the 32nd President of the United States, was visiting the Panama Canal Zone[1], and La Boca Elementary and Junior High School children were lined up along the La Boca route of the motorcade to wave little American flags as the president, dressed in a white Panama suit and hat, drove by in a big black open limousine. James was the most conspicuously energetic flag waver in his entire class that day, waving two flags and you might have thought he was the head of the flag waving committee, and that the President was waving back especially to him in acknowledgment and appreciation.

His experience in the first and second grades, though, from the beginning was not too pleasant, because he was very insecure and not used to being still for long periods of time. He simply acted as any insecure six-year-old would do to get attention. In fact, when he saw that it was easier to be a clown and make other children laugh, or do pranks to get them to notice him, that is exactly what he did. He got away with it, too, in the first grade perhaps because his first-grade teacher, Ms. Dawkins, was a most patient Mother Theresa type; but when he advanced to the second grade and he attempted that same behavior, his second-grade teacher, Ms. Whyte, a strict disciplinarian, would have none of it. The first time he did his pranks and clowning he got her attention, and she didn't hesitate to inflict dire punishment on him right before the class by pinching the Lucifer out of him and twisting his ears which he didn't enjoy, and, in fact, it was quite painful. After reports reached home and a couple of visits were made to the school by his mother, who further embarrassed him in front of the class with a half dozen slaps behind his head and additional ear twisting, and, after he found less painful ways of getting attention and making friends, his behavior improved to the delight of everyone, especially the teacher, and there was no more need for emergency visits. (When it comes to school, West Indians don't play. They don't believe in all that child psychology business. They have a saying, 'Yuh spare the rod, yuh goin' spoil the chile,' or something like that.)

Going on six to seven years old, he was most attracted to the many street vendors who came through La Boca town almost every day, like the 'old gol' man buying old trinkets and jewelry made of gold; the 'old rag man' buying old rags and clothes used for reprocessing to make something useful out of; like the raspado vendor who sold shaved ice in sugar cones with syrup on it; and the fresh-baked bread and pastry vendor, Mr. Haynes (whom children loved), with the finest tenor voice calling out from the street early in the morning, "Come and get your morning bread, your morning bread, get out your bed and get your bread..." and he kept the freshest, warmest pastry inside a glass case on wheels; and there was the coconut vendor, Mr. Gaston, a stocky Frenchman from Martinique with a thick moustache and a heavy French accent who used to set up his four-wheel pushcart every day on Martinique Street in front of the bachelor quarters near the commissary by the intersection of Martinique Street and Barbados Street, to catch as many passersby as possible. Where he got so many coconuts from James did not know; perhaps he had a coconut farm somewhere, maybe in the interior. Nevertheless, Mr. Gaston knew James' parents well and James often went by and helped him with his coconut business by cleaning up the thrash and throwing stuff away and he used to admire how adeptly that Frenchman would slice off the top of each coconut, swiiisssssh, with one swipe of that sharp machete of his. But the best part of all was that James could drink all the coconut water and eat all the coconut jelly he wanted. Then there was, lastly, the charcoal vendor, that enigmatic little charcoal vendor with his pushcart from Chorrillo. There is a very intriguing story that goes with that vendor, too.

When James was seven years old, he was very curious about everything including the mystery of charcoal. He used to wonder where it came from and why it was so black and powdery, odorless, and if it got on your hands or clothes, you had such a hard time cleaning it off. He had once thought that by burning a piece of wood the black ash that was left in the fire was charcoal and he couldn't see how that could be useful to anyone, but it wasn't that simple as he later learned in the Jr. high school. He learned that wood and all organic matter had to be treated within the earth by Mother Nature in a special way over a long, long period of time before being converted to charcoal. At seven he knew that people used it to cook in their coal pot stoves before kerosene stoves became popular, and that charcoal burned long and slowly and gave off a lot of heat. He had even seen a coal pot stove once in his mother's kitchen. It seemed like in the early days everybody had one at one time because the charcoal vendor used to make a good living selling charcoal when he and his two sons, or helpers, came through the streets of La Boca pushing a big 4-wheel cart full of it all the way across the border from Chorillo, Panama. He had a gong that he would beat with a hammer or a piece of metal bar, bong, bong, bong, two or three times, and then he would call out from the street: "CAAARRRBBOOONNN….COOOOOAAAL….COOOOOAAA

L.... bong, bong, bong..." With his clothes all sooty and soiled, he would weigh the coal on a crude scale as he portioned it out to sell it by the pound to customers. He was a short man about 5 feet tall and what stood out most about him was his head. He had a very big head for his size, so they called him, "Cabezon, Cabezon Grande." One day James got brave enough to join in with the older boys who were teasing the charcoal vendor as they called out to him, 'CABEZON!!!... CABEZON GRANDE!!!... Now, he never liked it when they called him that name, so he chased after them with a piece of stick or metal rod cursing at them in Spanish: "Cabrones... cabrones..." James couldn't run as fast as the older boys and Cabezon was right on his tail. If he hadn't run under the cellar by Mr. Lashley, who was there at the time working in his workshop, and then dashed upstairs by the back staircase, Cabezon, who backed off when he saw Mr. Lashley with some sharp tools in his hands, would have caught one little frightened brat and who knows what would have happened to him because that vendor was mad as a rabid dog. When James got upstairs shaking like a scared rabbit, he never came downstairs again for the rest of that day.

Another incident occurred when he was still 7. At that time his parents lived in house #1032, San Domingo Street, on the second floor (which really was as high as a third floor if you consider that the house was built high above the ground level on posts about 6 feet tall, so if you considered the "cellar" like a ground floor then the 1st floor was like a second floor and the 2nd floor was as high as a regular 3rd floor.) Anyway, that gives you a sense of how high the 2nd floor really was. On the 2nd floor, therefore, lived 6 families. One of the families was the Bests, Reginald and Edith Best from Barbados. They had a daughter, Eldika, who had a son, Sam, Jr., no more than 5 years old. In 1935 the front porch overlooking San Domingo Street had a guard wall built up to 5 feet high from the floor so that there was nothing but open space above it, between the top of the guard wall and the ceiling, which allowed you to look out from the 2nd floor unobstructed. It was taken for granted, but it was really dangerous if you leaned too far over the edge -- there was nothing to prevent you from falling 50 feet to the ground below. One day children were playing in the street and since little Sammy was not allowed to go downstairs, he was looking out over the ledge to see the children downstairs playing. He must have stood on a box and leaned too far over at the moment when Eldika was not paying attention to him, and he lost his balance and fell 50 feet headfirst to the ground below. It was a tragedy! Eldika lost her mind and Edith ran downstairs and picked the lifeless body up and brought it upstairs crying profusely and praying desperately. She rubbed him with every kind of healing ointment you could think of, with smelling salts, alcohol, bay rum, aloe, and cradled him in her arms while sobbing pitifully, but it was no use, they could not revive him, and he died in her arms. It was such a sorrowful thing to see, especially for James, a 7-year-old! And you know, after that day they came and put up a wire screen covering the entire open space of the balcony from the ledge of the guard wall to the ceiling above so that nothing or no one could fall over that balcony ledge ever again...but of course, it was too late for poor little Sammy.

When James was 8 years old, they took him to visit his paternal grandmother, Mama Bulow, who was 95 years old at the time, very sick and being cared for in Ancon Hospital until they transferred her in 1936 to another hospital called Matias Hernandez in Panama City. When she was young, Mama Bulow remarried to Papa Bulow, a French man, and they lived in Chorrillo after her Jamaican husband, James' biological grandfather, left her with three children in Panama City and returned to Jamaica at the time of the French Canal fiasco. James still believes to this day that after his tired, overworked grandmother (born in Martinique in 1841) had coped with more than her share of hardships in this world, at 95 years old it was no wonder that she had lost her mental acuity. It was even more amazing to James that she had lived that long, much less with any faculties left, as he saw her cringe away, afraid and unaware of who we were, until Mr. Edwards, her son, comforted her and calmed her down. Anyway, as an 8-year-old, James' little soul was so moved when he saw her in such a feeble, demented condition, he cried. A few years after that visit, Mama Bulow passed away.

Later In the year 1936, James and a group of small boys, averaging 8-12 years old, were running around inside the clubhouse basement where they had a hairdressing parlor, a barbershop, a typing class, and a poolroom. Many days these boys would hang around the clubhouse, which was a popular community center with a movie theatre on the second floor, a restaurant on the first floor, and a long wing extension attached to, and leading from, the back of the first floor, consisting of several meeting rooms and reading rooms. Anyway, the basement, and especially the poolroom, was the favorite place for pool and billiard lovers; and the little boys not old enough to be allowed to shoot pool, but who hung around the poolroom, were a nuisance to the older boys who were allowed to play. One day some bigger boys were playing pool and they had some money bet on the game when the nuisance kids came bursting into the room, and no amount of warning could scare them or get them to clear out and find someplace else to play. "Boyer", one of the older boys, was about to make a difficult shot when suddenly "Papsy", the wildest little troublemaker in the group, ran into Boyer and made him miss the shot. Boyer had warned him before, but he was daring and hard-of-hearing, so this time Boyer was going to teach him a lesson. He swung the cue stick with all his might at Papsy and hit him squarely in his temple, "BAM". The blow was hard and knocked Papsy down off his feet; but in a few seconds he got up and mimicked Boyer and ran away. When his companions asked him if he was alright, he laughed it off, "Ah, that was nothing; I'm alright," and they kept on playing. Later that evening when they all went home, Papsy complained about a little headache and his mother, Mrs. Brown, sent him to lie down, but he didn't tell her what had happened in the poolroom. The next morning when they tried to wake him up it was too late for poor Papsy. By the time they got him to the hospital he died from a massive brain hemorrhage due to the trauma to his head caused by the blow. His companions learned a serious lesson that day.

When James was 8 going on 9 and old enough to count and be responsible for making small purchases by himself, especially on Sunday afternoons when the commissary was closed, his parents would send him to the Chinese garden across the "Main", La Boca Road, to the Chinese shop with a quarter to buy 5c worth of lucky strikes for his dad, 10c worth of cooking oil for his mom who sometimes ran short, and 5c worth of lettuce (and he'd better bring back the correct change when he came home if he knew what was good for him). He didn't mind doing the errand and Mrs. Edwards would take good care and wrap the quarter up in a good size piece of brown paper and pin it inside his pocket so it wouldn't get lost by accident. He walked from one end of La Boca to the Main Street and crossed the Main to reach the Chinese shop. The Chinese man was good enough to help him unpin the money from his pocket and parcel out the items carefully after counting and weighing them, "one," "two," "three," "four," "five" cigarettes at 1c apiece; a small bunch of freshly picked lettuce at 5c (which he wrapped and placed in a Chinese bag); and 8oz. of cooking oil for 10c which they had poured out already. But the best part of all, the "pesuna", was what James really came there for. It is a treat that you get from the Chinese as a bonus – a piece of wrap-a-duro (hardened molasses or hardened brown sugar that James loved and would walk a mile for.) The Chinese man made sure he neatly wrapped the change (5c) in the brown paper and pinned it back in James' pocket and sent him home with his packages.

By this time James had a huge crop of hair on his head. His mother had let his hair grow so bushy and long that the neighborhood boys and girls teased him and said he was starving the barber. His mother decided to spare him any further peer humiliation by escorting him one day to the clubhouse barbershop and had barber Joe cut off his hair so close that it gave him such a clean, shiny baldhead that made his head feel cool and naked until he believed, to this day, that that was what started him wearing headgear to shield his head from the elements.

When he was almost 9 years old, he remembers an incident that took place when the boys in his neighborhood used to form little gangs and engage in pranks, like ringing people's doorbells and raiding people's gardens. (Many West Indians loved to cultivate vegetables, grow cane and corn and bananas in gardens in front of or near their homes. One famous West Indian named Buck Jones had a good size garden between the outfield of La Boca ball ground and the oil tank farm in the eastern part of La Boca. He would go there every day and do work in his garden until late, except on Saturdays and Sundays. Nobody messed with him because Buck Jones was a mean man you didn't mess with. He almost killed a man once with his machete. The man had trespassed into his fenced-off garden with a "No Trespassing" sign on it.

That man begged for his life till he almost wet himself. Those boys of James' age or a little older weren't afraid of anybody, though, and loved to take chances. So, they decided one day for excitement they were going to raid Buck Jones' garden. It was on a Saturday afternoon around 4 p.m. when they thought B. J. had finished work early and had left and gone home, which they observed him do on previous Saturdays and Sundays. So, after checking carefully to make sure that B. J. was not there, they decided to break through the fence and vandalize the place. There was no money to steal, just some bananas in the trees that seemed inviting and maybe they could steal some cane and corn by the time they got through. They grabbed first a bunch of bananas and gave them to Pappy Kellman to hold and wait till they went in further while he stood at the lookout post near the entrance until they returned. But they miscalculated! Buck Jones did not go home early, and he was waiting for them as they came after the cane and corn patch. They scrambled out of there yelling at the top of their lungs, "run," "run for your lives". Pappy didn't wait when he heard them, and he took off with the bunch of bananas and ran as fast as he could. Since he had a head start nobody was going to catch him. He got back to their hangout under house 1078 before everybody else and when the others reached, lucky to be alive, the first thing they said was, "Where is Pappy?" They knew he got away and was the first one back, but he was nowhere to be found. They knew he had the bunch of bananas, too, so they waited to find him to split up the bunch, 4 guys, 24 bananas, 6 apiece; but they couldn't find Pappy. They were mad as hell. They were planning when they found him what they were going to do to him. It was getting late by then so they decided they would see him the next day. The next day when he didn't come downstairs to play, they called to Mrs. Kellman, "Isn't Pappy coming downstairs to play with his friends today?" "No," replied Mrs. Kellman, "Pappy can't come downstairs, Pappy has got cholic; he sick bad, he ate 24 green bananas. He can't come downstairs to play." And the boys didn't know whether to laugh at him or hate Pappy. "He ate all 24 bananas, most of them green, all by himself. Good for him; bet he don't eat no more bananas after today," they said, "especially green ones." After a while they all got over it and for a long time Pappy was the subject of the best joke --- 24 green bananas!

When he was 7 James' older brother, Charles, had a part-time job working for the Secretary of the La Boca clubhouse. The secretary was an African American named Mr. Williams who lived on "Gold" Street near the ballpark in one of the few two-family low houses in la Boca. His brother's job was to do a few chores in Mr. and Mrs. Williams' house and around the yard in the evenings after school (like emptying out the garbage, etc.). One of his rewards was a free pass to go to the movies in la Boca clubhouse theatre anytime he wanted, and he could even take his little brother, James, along. Wow! This meant they could see all the best movies that came to La Boca movie theatre in those days, especially on Friday nights when they were showing "serials" like Buck Jones, The Lone Ranger, Charlie Chan, Fu Man Chu and shorts featuring the Nicholas Brothers, the Harlem Globe Trotters, and Lena Horne, etc. Whenever they showed a Joe Louis fight, though, it was almost impossible even for the two of them to get a seat. The theatre was so crowded on those nights that they had to use the back of the theatre's two-flight emergency exit to let people in and out after the showing of each movie before the next show that evening could start. Since the staircase had hardly ever been used before, it was very fragile and shaky, and they almost had a serious accident one night when the crowd started pushing from behind. Fortunately, no fatalities occurred. As far as the free movie arrangement was concerned, for James and his brother it was a good thing while it lasted, and it lasted until Mr. Williams was recalled to the U.S. about two years later.

There is an interesting story about the man who replaced Mr. Williams as the secretary of La Boca clubhouse. He was another African American named Mr. Neely. He was a mean, cold-hearted man who smoked a stinking Cuban cigar and who spoke with a heavy American accent. You couldn't get away with anything around him for too long. Mr. Tudor, a Barbadian, worked for the clubhouse division and at nights his job was to collect theatre admission tickets at the door from everyone going to the movies. Tudor was a nice man, square jawed, never smoked a day in his life and always had a toothpick in his mouth.

He was also Darnley Tudor's father and Darnley could go to the movies free every night because he was Tudor's kid. Now, Mr. Tudor had a nice little racket going on the side for himself. The ticket fare was a dime for children and a quarter for adults and you had to buy the tickets in advance at the ticket window before going upstairs into the theatre. You would hand the ticket to Mr. Tudor who sat at the foot of the stairs and would tear the ticket in half, give you a half and deposit the other half in a box near him. Everybody who knew what was going on, knew that you could avoid paying the full fare by handing off a nickel, dime or fifteen cents in cash at the foot of the stairs to Mr. Tudor who would pocket it and let you enter without having to buy a ticket for the full price, and that way he subsidized his salary. This went on for quite a while before Mr. Neely caught on. One day Mr. Neely gave Tudor the night off and decided that he was going to stand, or sit, at the entrance and collect tickets himself that night. He stood at the foot of the stairs and as people passed him, they handed him their tickets. That night they had a big double feature and everybody and his cousin was going to the movies. The light was a little dim and one by one the scammers came and dropped a dime or fifteen cents into Mr. Neely's hand thinking the scam was still on and went past him up the stairs into the theatre. He kept quiet for a while, kept track of it, saving the evidence, and was very, very angry. But he was angry most of all when up there came Darnley Tudor and he tried to get by Mr. Neely without paying. As he ran up the stairs he said the magic words, "Tudor kid, Tudor Kid," and that took the cake. Mr. Neely stopped him in his tracks and yelled at him: "Git back down hyar niggar!!!...you could be Tudah kid, or you could be Tudah goat, man, man, git ta hell out o' hyar!!!" And that was the end of Mr. Tudor's scam and his job as a movie ticket collector as well.

There were other incidents, of course, like the time in June 1937 when James was 9 years old and there was a partial eclipse of the sun around 3 o'clock in the afternoon. Everybody was waiting to see how dark it would get when the moon, as they said, blocked out the sun. Since you couldn't look directly at the sun, all the children were burning pieces of plain glass in the fire to char it black so you could look through it without getting blinded. Anyway, only about two-thirds of the sun was blocked from view by the moon so the place wasn't as dark as it would have been if it were a total eclipse. It made for good conversation, though, the next day in school.

Also, in 1937, when he was in the fourth grade and Panama was completing the construction of the new Olympic Stadium in preparation for hosting the 1938 Central American Olympics[2], every evening after school and on weekends he would join the crowds who came out to La Boca ball park to watch the future Olympians like Jennings Blackett, Wesley Chevannes, John West, Frank Prince, Nola Thorne, Lilia Wilson, and others practice and train. Besides preparing to qualify for the Olympics, they were also members of the La Boca School athletic program coached by Aston M. Parchment (Many other future athletes like Clayton Clarke, Cyril McSween, Delores Worrel, Rica Hobbs, Seymour Lashley, Lenie Alexander etc. would come under Parchment's tutelage and would go on to excel in the 1946 and 1950 Olympics in Baranquilla, Columbia and in Guatemala City, Guatemala respectively). When the February, 1938 Olympics took place in Panama City, many of the above-mentioned Panamanian-West Indian stars competed in it and made their families, communities, and the Republic of Panama proud of them. In every competition Panamanian-West Indians did well, but especially in track and field they carried away the gold and silver medals. Nola Thorne and Jennings Blackett – the two fastest track stars in the 1938 Olympics respectively won the 80-meter hurdles, 100- meter dash, 100-meter relay, men's 100 meters, 200 meters and 100 meters relay races. Jennings Gordon Blackett was so fast that he shattered the games 100-meter record of 10:7 with a time of 10:3 and was called by the Panamanians "El humano el mas veloz del mundo (the fastest man alive – literally, the fastest human being in the world.)" He had tied the world record at that time.

It is no wonder the "silver" communities in those days produced so many fine athletes. It is true that West Indian athletes had exceptional natural ability, but their success was due largely to their school's fine athletic program. In the Silver communities they used to have intramural and inter school sports competition every year. In the intramural meets at La Boca School, for example, the whole school attended the meets on the ball ground and rooted for their individual classes and their favorite athletes. When

James was in the 5th grade, he represented his class by running in the 200-meter race. On that occasion when they reached to the half-way mark on the tracks, he was in clear first place and looked like he was a sure winner running away with the race; but, unfortunately, the other runners caught up with him and passed him by before he reached the tape. He kept looking back to see where the other runners were and each time when he looked back, more of them passed him by, until he was the last one left. That was the end of his Olympic aspirations. He never ran again after that; he was too embarrassed.

Aside from the Olympics, La Boca town was truly a sports town. In fact, most silver towns were. Besides track and field, they had a softball league, baseball league, cricket league, a soccer league, a Canal Zone divisional league (the mechanical, electrical, commissary, transportation division, etc.) and teams competed against other teams in inter-divisional, inter-school, inter-town competitions travelling, on alternating schedules, to each other's community ballparks. (Sometimes the competition was so fierce, and tempers were so high, that after a hard-fought grudge game if the visiting team was the winning team, they were lucky to get out of town in one piece). It was, however, stellar entertainment for the town spectators who came out in the dry season

(December to April) and filled up the grandstands and lined up along the tracks to enjoy seeing the youths show off their skills. The only sport that was popular in the rainy season (May to November) was soccer, a mud-and-guts game. La Boca even had an outdoor basketball court in front of the school at one time. So, when the Republic of Panama started their professional baseball league, basketball league or any kind of national professional league, including professional boxing, wrestling and tennis, there was no difficulty finding West Indian talent from the Canal Zone. Just like in track and field, they excelled in every sport in Panama. These, then, were some of the highlights and events of James Edwards' early childhood years recalled by him on many occasions.

Chapter II:

Hard Realities

August 15, 1938, marked the twenty-fourth year of the opening of the Panama Canal and Afro-Panamanians made up the largest ethnic population in Colon and Panama City. First- generation West Indians (criollos) born in Panama and the Canal Zone had come of age by that time while second-generation offspring, like James, were still in their childhood or early adolescent stage. In those days when you heard Americans talk about the Canal, they would boast as if it was their canal, their pride and joy, like the land belonged to them and they had every right to occupy the Canal Zone and regard it as United States territory, which was no surprise since the 1903 treaty between the U.S. and Panama practically gave them sovereignty over the C.Z. into perpetuity; and they all but safeguarded and protected it zealously as theirs with their own police force and military to back them up. Aside from the numerous U. S. army, navy, and air force installations and forts located in strategic locations throughout the Isthmus of Panama, there were more than seventeen civilian towns under United States jurisdiction that existed within the Canal Zone that stretched 5 miles on each side of the

Canal itself along its 50-mile length across the Isthmus from the Pacific to the Atlantic Ocean. In the Atlantic side Canal Zone there were three gold (white) towns: Cristobal, Coco Solo, Margarita and four silver (black) towns: Silver City, Silver City Heights, Camp Coiner, Gatun; and on the Pacific side there were six gold towns: Gamboa, Pedro Miguel, Diablo Heights, Curundu, Ancon, Balboa (where the Canal Zone administration was located on a hill called **Balboa Heights)** and four silver towns: Gamboa (or Santa Cruz), Paraiso, Red Tank and La Boca. The nearest silver town to the Atlantic Ocean was Silver City in the province of Colon and the nearest silver town to the Pacific Ocean was La Boca in the province of Panama City.

When these towns were built by the U. S. with permanent housing for the Canal Zone civilian workforce and their families, they were separated systematically by race with Blacks assigned to "silver towns" with inferior and overcrowded wooden tenements. The largest known tenement building was in the town of Red Tank and it was called the "Titanic" because it housed 48 families. Also, in La Boca, where James Edwards was born, they had a Titanic and a Britannic building, each with 20 or more families living them. White people, on the other hand, were assigned to "gold towns" with luxurious and spacious living quarters in 2- and 4-family houses some of which were made of concrete with laundry and maid facilities attached. The populations were forced to adhere to strict social barriers and taboos that were codified and inscribed in signs and posters at the entrance of common public facilities (post offices, churches, hospitals, trains, and wherever there were bathrooms and drinking fountains in public places). On the Canal Zone the races were not allowed to mix, and the strictest laws and racial codes were enforced by a segregated Canal Zone police force (which included black policemen whose authority was limited to patrolling only the silver towns; and they had no power to arrest white people and were lower in rank and pay than white officers).

West Indians in the Canal Zone were limited to far fewer privileges and benefits than whites and were powerless against white authority -- in fact, they were dealt with severely whenever they stood their ground against unfair treatment (In many cases they were fired without due process, evicted, and even "blackballed" from the Canal Zone). Black people were restricted to inferior and inadequate housing for which they had to pay rent, unlike whites who lived rent-free in far superior dwellings; blacks were limited to segregated, inferior colored schools for their children who were only permitted to advance as far as the 7th, later the 8th grade, while the whites had senior high schools and junior colleges; and blacks were limited to commissary privileges in segregated, inferior stocked "silver" commissaries. Both white and black communities were provided free services such as sanitation, garbage collection, security, maintenance, health, etc. by the authoritarian government that owned and strictly controlled and regulated everything in the Canal Zone (They even took an official census in every household periodically to account for every being who lived in them); and, lastly, West Indians were dealt perhaps the most egregious indignity by being paid insultingly lower wages[3&4]. Black workers were on a "silver roll" pay scale ($22.50 - $80.00)/mo. while white workers were paid on a "gold roll" pay scale ($105.00 - $375.00)/mo. with the average white salary $372.00/mo. including a 50% overseas differential compensation which was added in and which they all received in addition to their regular salary (Later the 50% was reduced to 25%). Moreover, white workers received 24 days cumulative annual leave up to a maximum of 120 days and a guaranteed pension, free roundtrips to their homelands in the United States annually for each worker and their immediate families, plus sick leave and free transportation on the railroad, while the average black employee's salary was $51.25/mo. with no pension, no overseas differential compensation, no free round trips to their homelands annually, no free transportation on the Panama Railroad, etc.

On a salary of $55.00/mo. Richard Edwards, James' father, who was the son of an ex-digger who had worked for the French Canal Company before it finally went bankrupt in 1894, was employed by the United States Panama Canal Commission when the U. S. took over the construction of the Canal in 1904. He was a seaman for the Dredging Division and when the Thatcher ferry began operations in 1932, carrying traffic to and from the west and east banks of the canal near the town of La Boca, he was assigned as a ferry operator to work a rotating shift (3-11, 11-7, and 7-3) five days a week on the Thatcher ferry directing traffic. It was convenient because he could now walk from his home in La Boca to his job in less than a half hour.

Many a time after work or on his days off he could be seen trekking up Far Fan Hill on the west bank of the ferry (facing the Pacific Ocean) to his little free farm on some free land on the hillside where he, like many other West Indian workers, cultivated earth food like yams, cocoa, yucca, sweet potatoes, yampis, green plantains and green bananas to feed the family. Occasionally he would catch an armadillo in the wild that would provide enough meat for one or two days. James recalled that on many Saturdays he and his two older brothers would accompany their father to his farm to help with the cultivating and harvesting. On some of those occasions his brothers would encourage him to climb down with them on the opposite, bushier backside of the hill onto the sands of Hideaway beach, the beach where West Indians were allowed to swim as opposed to the white beach not far away called Far Fan beach that was off-limits to blacks. They would hurry and climb back up the bushy hill before it was time to return home with their father.

At other times on the hillside when they had a rest break from digging the soil up to clear and plant or harvest earth food, they would sit and look out at the beautiful Pacific Ocean and see ships entering or leaving the Canal and try their best to name them and the country they were from. They also enjoyed looking across the east bank at their hometown of La Boca to see if they could recognize people and the houses where they lived. After these breaks, they would return to their farming chores on the hillside. When it was time for the crops to be harvested, Mr. Edwards and his three sons would fill up several large burlap (crocus) bags with all the earth food they could gather: yellow yams, white yams, yuccas, cocoas, sweet potatoes, yampies, green plantains, green bananas, and carry them on their backs down the hillside across the ferry back home to La Boca town. It was a sight to see when they laid it all out on the floor and separated it out into portions to give to each of their neighbors in house #1032, for they always shared their produce with their neighbors at harvest time.

Chapter III:

Adolescent Years

By 1939 James Edwards had reached his 11th birthday, he was the youngest of five surviving children in the Edwards' household, a student in the 6th grade at La Boca Elementary School and in the grips of his pre-teen years. His pastime consisted mostly of neighborhood adventures and pranks, playing softball with other youth on the school grounds or in the La Boca ballpark every evening after school when it didn't rain, or flying kites near the seashore on windy days or going swimming in their favorite beach hideout called "Calmetto" in the Pacific Ocean behind the school. In the rainy season they would play soccer and stick-in-the-mud, sail paper boats in the street gutters which they loved to do when the rainwater would swell and then slowly run off in the gutters after heavy rains, or they would play marbles under the "cellars" of most houses. At this stage in life, he wasn't so keen on doing homework or chasing after girls; but gradually he found that he was growing taller, his voice was changing, hormones acting up and he was turning into an adolescent. Suddenly he was not a 6th grader anymore; he was thrust into the 7th grade where he now faced the insecurities that come with transitioning from childhood to adolescence and it overwhelmed him. He had to shed the comforts of his juvenile behavior patterns for more mature ones which at first wasn't easy to do, so he looked around for male role models.

In those days there were many adult males in the community but not all were good role models to follow. For example, there was Mr. Cumberbatch, "The Bull", who was a black cop dressed in khaki uniform who patrolled La Boca and drove fear into young men who liked to gamble under the cellars. Sometimes he sneaked up on them and as they ran away leaving all their money on the ground behind them, the Bull would snatch it up and go on his merry way with his four pockets bulging. But he wasn't a good role model because of that and because he later got a bad reputation for other sinister things he supposedly did, like scaring ladies at night. Then there was Herbie Bascombe, a muscular, mean-looking 6.3-ft young man who lived in a first-floor apartment in house #1030 on San Domingo Street. He not only scared other youths, he scared animals, too, even rabid dogs. He was seen grabbing a rabid dog one day and ringing its neck till it broke. He could catch a pigeon in flight and flip its head off with his thumb. Everybody feared him and wouldn't dare to challenge

Herbie in a fight... he was so mean and cruel, although he was one of the best roller skaters in La Boca. He used to jump clear over dozens of bodies lying side by side in the street and he never even scratched a soul. But he wasn't a good role model, no sir!

And there was Wilfred "Putty Knife" Lynch. He was a hustler and a gambler, always gambling with cards and dice under the cellars. He was cold, always carried a putty knife for protection and used to bully smaller boys, like the time when he beat up Leon Harper and Mr. Harper, a famous "stickman" had to teach him a lesson by beating him up bad with his famous "stick-of-war" one day in La Boca Clubhouse poolroom. He didn't convert after he got that licking, he only got meaner with everybody else -- but he was scared from then on when he saw Mr. Harper, and he never messed with Leon again. Putty Knife was not a good role model either, neither were the "chance men" who sold numbers that played at 11 o'clock every Sunday in the Panama lottery and who were always just one step away from getting arrested by the police for selling clandestine lottery ("chance"), nor were the men who loved the bottle (They drank a lot of "murf" - raw alcohol mixed with prunes and cloves and buried in the earth for a time to ferment), nor were the men who were loafers and who were women chasers.

However, there were many examples of good role models to follow. The first one James turned to of course was his father, Richard Edwards, a good ghost storyteller, and a fluent speaker of 4 languages (English, Spanish, French, and Patois) even though he only went as far as the 4th grade in school. More important, he was a hardworking family provider and a devoted husband and father. He even took in homeless youths on separate occasions over the years (Can you imagine that, with an underpaid West Indian worker's pay!! He and his wife, Marie were truly caring and unselfish!) It was natural that sometimes married couples would have disagreements. They had an understanding that when it came to talking out disagreements between them that they didn't want their children to know about, they were to only speak in French or Patois. James could tell you that when his parents were discussing any "grown up (private) business" that they didn't want their children to know about, the "Patois" would fly and, if that didn't work, then the "French" would fly! There was an awful lot of patois spoken in the house sometimes and it sounded like cussing to James because he didn't understand a word they were saying. As far as discipline was concerned, Mr. Edwards didn't always use the strap, sometimes he used psychology. James could attest to that fact because when he and his next older brother were 9 and 11 respectively and had missed curfew (9 o'clock) one too many times and came home late at night, Mr. Edwards dealt with that problem in a very unique way. He would tell them ghost stories that scared the "bejeezuz" out of them. He would tell them about seeing weird ghosts in the streets of La Boca late at night when he was coming home from work and that there was a certain ghost who liked to stand on the street corner a few blocks away from their house. This ghost would be playing a guitar and he stood about 6 - 8 inches off the ground with his hair standing straight up and with sharp pointed teeth, and it was no use trying to run from him because if you tried to run, by the time you reached to the next block he was already there waiting for you. "I was lucky," said Mr. Edwards, "that when he asked me for a cigarette, I had one to give him; but when I saw the smoke coming out of his ears, that scared even me." Without any further details, James and his older brother Charles never missed curfew again after that.

The next role model James turned to was Mr. Hubert Lord, a Barbadian painter and a remarkable boat builder who, like James' father (and most West Indians), didn't graduate from high school, but was skillful with his hands, could read blueprints and build large boats in his spare time. You would see him under house #1073 in the evenings after work singlehandedly building beautiful 15-ft boats that would amaze James. James also turned to Mr. Charles Jones, whose family lived directly beneath the Edwards in house #1032. Mr. Jones was a talented carpenter and furniture maker who came from Barbados and who worked in construction. In his spare time, he would build the most beautiful furniture you could ever imagine, such as armoirs, dressers, wardrobes, cabinets, etc. and James, while playing marbles "under the cellar" of house 1032, would often stop just to admire the work of this craftsman as he "planed" and sanded so smooth the finished pieces and stained and shellacked them. James swore that the finished work looked better than anything he saw in the furniture stores in Panama City. Mrs. Jones never had to worry in the least about dressing up her apartment with any kind of furniture she wanted. Then there was Mr. Cyril Dacosta Lashley, a skilled Barbadian tinsmith and metalworker who single-handedly built (in his workshop under the cellar) most of the two- and three- burner tin kerosene stoves in the neighborhood; his workmanship was known all over La Boca. Then there was Mr. Roach, the best shoemaker in the Panama Canal Zone. James could tell you how many half soles and worn-out heels Mr. Roach, the shoemaker, replaced for him and for the entire town.

Finally, as he advanced in school, James turned to his Jr. High School principal and teachers for role models. Though at first he had reservations about principal Morgan, because he always stood on the front steps of the school building with a thick strap waiting to welt you with it as you passed by if you were late, James came to gain a great deal of respect for him after he found out that A. L. B. Morgan was a war hero[5] who had served as a Company Quartermaster Sergeant in the British regiment in Egypt and Palestine during W. W. I. and he was honorably discharged. Then, he came to the Isthmus where he was employed as a teacher in 1921 and taught every grade there is in the colored elementary and junior high schools with commendation, before he was promoted to Assistant Principal of Silver City colored School; and in 1933 he was again promoted to Principal of La Boca colored School when he took Mr. S. K. Walters place who had retired. Although he wielded a strap and was a strict disciplinarian, he was also very fair-minded and dedicated to the students, faculty, and school. In 1944 he was transferred to Gamboa Elementary School to replace principal D. A. Osborne who had retired.

Another Junior High role model was Robert H. Beecher (who later earned a B.A. from Michigan U. and a PhD from NYU). He was James' 7th grade social studies teacher, and was born in Gatun, C. Z. When he was a teenager his parents sent him away to Browns Town, Saint Ann, Jamaica, where he received his early schooling and his secondary education, returning to the Canal Zone to become a teacher in the junior high school, and, later, director of La Boca Junior College. He was always pursuing advanced studies both in Panama and the U. S. and achieved a doctorate degree from New York University. He was soft-spoken by nature, had a friendly smile and a drawl and was highly respected by his students and peers.

Next, there was Mr. Aston M. Parchment, a multi-talented, outstanding graduate of St. George College, Jamaica, a former famous Jamaican soccer star (goalkeeper) who became athletic and sports director of La Boca Jr. High School and who trained many star athletes who excelled in the Central American Olympics of 1938, 1946 and 1950. He also taught mathematics and was one of La Boca's outstanding community leaders who helped organize the INYC (Isthmian Negro Youth Congress).

Then there was Mr. Emile Benjamin, calm but mean and short tempered, a great wood-work teacher, a master carpenter who like Hubert Lord and Mr. Jones could build any wooden structure (even a house – he built the Normal School boys dormitory and also the high school building extension for the mechanic shop and printing shop attached to it), although he later lost sight in one eye (They say that it was due to an on-the-job accident that soured his temperament a bit).

Then there was James C. Webster who was a teacher back in Jamaica before migrating to Panama in 1910 and was hired to teach in the Canal Zone schools for youth that was established at the time in Cucaracha, Gorgona, Culebra, Empire, Mandingo, Matachin, Cruces, and Marajal, towns that were all later submerged in the Canal. In 1918 he became principal of Gatun School where he worked for 22 years. In 1940 he was transferred to Silver City elementary and Jr. High schools to succeed principal T. S. Johnston, then in 1944 he was transferred to La Boca Elementary and Jr. High School replacing A. L. B. Morgan; and, finally, in 1946 he was assigned to Red Tank Elementary School from where he retired. When the Division of Schools initiated pre-vocational training in the colored schools in the early nineteen thirties, he played a prominent part as Agricultural Science was his main forte, and he became an enthusiastic teacher of school gardening. He believed strongly in agriculture which along with bee raising had been his favorite hobby. In 1936 James Webster was awarded the Centenary Gold Medal by the

Miconian Association (Mico College) for meritorious service as a teacher, the first time Mico College honored one of its distinguished sons for achievement outside of Jamaica. He had given more than 35 years of service to the Panama Canal Zone schools. Students in La Boca School used to call him "Job," but I never knew why. I believe it had something to do with the Biblical connotation. Perhaps to them he had the same faith as Job, or Job was his favorite Bible character who he would often quote.

Another role model was Mr. Peter Samuel Martin, English teacher, affable and pleasant, always with a smile on his face, always walking with an umbrella even when it wasn't raining and was always dressed in a white linen suit and tie, greeting everyone he passed with a smile and a friendly "How-di-doo". He was a Christian Mission bible lay preacher, too, who graduated from a college in the West Indies and came to the Isthmus during the canal construction era. He was one of several pioneer teachers, like Mr. Webster, who taught in the old pre- Canal construction towns of Empire and Gorgona that are at the bottom of the Canal today.

At home when James' father asked him what he wanted to be when he grew up, the first thing that came to his mind was a preacher, but later, when he gave it more serious thought and he realized or he rationalized that in that profession preachers were not supposed to commit sins, he changed his mind and decided that he wanted to be a school teacher instead, so the perfect role model for him was still P. S. Martin, the dramatic English teacher. (As an adolescent his far-fetched way of thinking was that at least as a teacher he didn't have to swear off sin and he could always switch back later to being a preacher if he should change his mind or get purified.)

James' adjustment to the Junior High was hard in the beginning because it required much self-discipline and hard work to keep up with his studies, but thanks to the influence of his role models who were disciplinarians and excellent examples to follow, he applied himself with greater diligence. Peter S. Martin was very inspiring though he could get very emotional at times whenever he dramatized stories until his face would turn red like "red" pepper, especially while symbolically striking down some arch villain or wicked adversary with a fatal blow. His self-inflicted emotional pain, alone, would convey the severity of the blow. You would see that same red face often during English grammar classes whenever some misguided troublemaker misbehaved and disrupted his class. And he, being a preacher, it took an awful lot of mischief to get P.S. real angry, but sometimes it did.

"Whaaaam..." when he had had enough, and slammed his book down on the nearest desk. "Satan..., Beelzibub..." he would shout while pointing to the guilty person who made him lose his Christian temper, "Out...out...you devil...get out of my classroom forthwith..." and you would swear that it was St. Michael himself raising his sword to banish the demon out of Heaven.

A little fear and a great deal of admiration were two mixed emotions P. S. Martin evoked from James along with his fascination for his dramatic teaching style and his monologues. James, like most of his classmates, was a little fearful of coming to P.S.'s class unprepared, for his chastisement was something not to be desired. Ask Luther Franco, one of his classmates, who was a perpetual victim for coming to school and never doing his homework. One day in particular, remembers James, when Luther, who sat next to him, didn't have himself together (either he didn't sleep well or didn't have a good breakfast), he forgot all about his homework. When P. S. addressed him and asked him to give the present, past, and progressive tense of a difficult verb, he could not answer, and mumbled something that wasn't the answer. After P.S. repeated the question a few more times and didn't get the correct response, he had had it with Luther. "I know your aunt, and I know your family," P. S. just warming up said to him, "they are good people. I can't believe you bear their name! There must be a mistake! You are lazy!! You hear me? You are lazy!!! If I had my druthers with you, you know what I would do with you? I would feed you verbs for breakfast, verbs for lunch and verbs for dinner every day until they came out of your pores, you hear me!"

Poor Luther just had to sit there and take it like a man and pray that his aunt never hears about this. He was embarrassed but he had only himself to blame; everybody knows, you never come to P.S.'s class without doing your homework. Nevertheless, despite Luther's tragedy, James gained a lasting love for scripture, drama, and literature through this God-fearing English teacher.

In the Junior High School James continued to improve in most of his subjects, especially math, for in the eighth and ninth grades he found another role model, John A. Parchment, who was a graduate of Mico College, Kingston, Jamaica and father of Aston M. Parchment, previously cited. John A. was no taller than 5 feet but to James he was a giant and a wizard in the subject of mathematics. He was creative, patient, and masterful in unravelling so methodically the mysteries of mathematics to James. Before he was assigned to his class James had no love for the subject of algebra, but one day John A. Parchment unlocked a secret key that led him to understand concepts that before were impossible to learn, and he grew thirsty for more. He went home that day and from then every night he applied himself devotedly to his algebra book going through it from page to page, cover to cover, until he could solve every single algebra problem he encountered. He got an "A" average in math that year. By the time he finished the ninth grade, he was one of three students: Enrique Rosas, Maurice Heywood, and himself, who were cited by Principal A. L. B.*Morgan for being the three most improved students scholastically in the Junior High School that school year. Thanks to Peter S. Martin and John A. Parchment for that.

Speaking about role models, when James was in the ninth grade and his interest in algebra and mathematics started to peak, he met another role model who became a life-long friend, Alvin Roy Williams. Alvin and his brother, Eustace Williams, both attended the La Boca Normal School and were in the class of 1938. Alvin was a wizard in chess, checkers, bid whist, and bridge. In fact, he was the best player in those four sports in Panama at the time. His brother, Eustace, became a teacher after graduating, but Alvin did not. James could not understand why -- Alvin was the brightest and most gifted person he knew. Anyway, he took a job in

Panama with the Fuerza y Luz Company (Panama's equivalent to Spectrum).

Getting back to how Alvin became one of James' role models, one day a lady friend of Eustace asked James to deliver a letter to Eustice. Since Eustace and Alvin lived in the bachelor quarters, on the 2nd floor, of the La Boca restaurant located on La Boca Road, James went there to complete his errand. When he arrived, he was surprised to see many bachelors gathered around a table in the hallway playing chess. He was so fascinated he stopped to watch them and almost forgot about his errand. There was Alvin, seated, beating up all the other players who could not make him get up. You see, two players sat down to play, and the loser would get up. But nobody could beat him. That was the first time James became interested in the game of chess, and Alvin became his role model, his tutor, and his best friend.

James still remembers one of the thrills he experienced in those days. It was the time Alvin took him to visit his good friend, the Editor-in-Chief of the Panama Tribune, Sidney A. Young. James was very impressed later by this editor when he learned that he was born in Jamaica, came to Panama as a teenager, worked on the Canal Zone in 1916 as a messenger, became disillusioned with racism he encountered there, and, as a result, left the Canal

Zone for Panama never to return to the Canal Zone. He went to work in Panama as a "printer's devil" at the Central American Printing Company. He also worked as a mercantile clerk, and as a baker, and he played baseball and was the founder of the Isthmian Baseball League in 1918. An eye injury caused him to stop playing baseball. He became very active in, and was a very staunch supporter of, Isthmian scouting for years. In addition, in 1924 he became a proofreader, then assistant manager of the Central American News and from 1926-1928 was cable editor for the Panama American Newspaper where, with his influence, he became editor of its daily West Indian page that immediately took off with the West Indian community. In 1928, because the white owner of the paper would not pay him the same salary as a white editor, Sidney quit and formed his own weekly newspaper, the Panama Tribune, of which he was both owner and editor-in-chief. In 1928 Sidney A. Young published "Isthmian Echoes," a collection of articles, essays and stories dedicated to the unity, welfare, and progress of the West Indian community in the Republic of Panama as well as to the advancement of colored people throughout the world. For all these reasons, therefore, Sidney A. Young more than impressed James Edwards, and he, too, became one of James' future role models. However, in one area he fell short. Alvin Williams did not bring

James to visit Sidney Young solely for a social visit. The main reason he brought James there was to play chess. Sidney had invited them. He knew he couldn't beat Alvin, but he was sure he could beat this novice who was Alvin's protégé. But James did not disappoint his tutor that day, he beat Sidney in a chess match by a score of 6-1. And that was how James Edwards' chess career got started. Later, he won a few chess tournaments, thanks to his tutor and one of his best role models, Alvin Roy Williams.

Chapter IV:

1940-1950, a Decade of Turbulence and

Promise

The beginning of the decade of 1940-1950 was perhaps one of the most challenging times for West Indians in Panama. James Edwards was in his teen years, and he recalled how frantic and discouraged the adults in the town of La Boca, Canal Zone were when they talked about their situation and their future in the Republic of Panama. The Panama Canal Zone already was no paradise for them, having to deal with racial discrimination, and, added to that, in 1940 on the world stage there was a madman called Adolf Hitler who with his Nazi war machine was terrorizing and invading countries and embroiling all of Europe and the World into World War II, so that it wasn't long before the U.S. got involved when Japan, an ally of Germany, attacked Pearl Harbor on December 7, 1941, thus invading the U. S. Pacific Islands. In the Panama Canal Zone the war brought a lot of anxiety and insecurity with the U. S. fleet going back and forth in the Pacific theatre to confront the Japanese forces in the Pacific islands, with a lot of U.S. soldiers and sailors off the ships on shore leave running loose in Panama, and a hyped up Civilian Defense Corp in the Canal Zone engaged every day in drills and "blackouts" and precautions that were scaring everybody as if the Japanese and the Germans were right on the border about to attack the Panama Canal at any minute (which thankfully never happened).

By 1942 when he was in the 8th grade, everyday James and his junior high school classmates could be heard talking about the news and could be seen exchanging war pictures extracted from the comic sections of the daily newspapers. The war was like a game to them as they compared the different battles on land, sea and in the air and talked about the generals and heroes like generals McArthur, Eisenhower, Montgomery, Patton, and the most famous German general Erwin Rommel (the desert fox). Of course, they knew about Doris "Dorie" Miller, the first African American hero and Navy Cross medal winner who died in the battle of Pearl Harbor[6]. They even used to make wooden miniature airplanes (P-40's and p-38's) in carpentry class and those classmates who had artistic ability (like Harold Scott, the 6' 6" giant, and James Edwards) could be seen often in art classes drawing pictures of tanks, airplanes, battleships, scenes of famous battles, and it was always fun to look through the classroom windows facing the Pacific Ocean to see the gray U.S.

fleet of ships lined up waiting to pass through the Panama Canal.

To young teenagers this was all very exciting but, in retrospect, the early 1940's was one of the worst periods for West Indians in Panama and in the Canal Zone, not so much because of the war or the blight of racial discrimination in the Panama Canal Zone, but mainly because the Panamanians in 1940 had elected Arnulfo Arias Madrid as their 10th President of the Republic of Panama and, in a very short time (1941), he had written a new constitution that wreaked havoc on West Indians and other immigrants in the country[7]. He was also a devoted Nazi (Hitler) admirer; he had no regard for West Indians and in his new constitution he denationalized 50,000 people and left them without a country, affecting their ability to travel, to obtain passports and legal documents. The "Nationalization of Commerce and Commercial Carnet Laws" in his constitution prohibited immigrants from running retail businesses and owning properties and resulted in many prosperous West Indians, small shop owners, doctors, lawyers, dentists, newspapermen, and businessmen being nearly ruined. By the end of 1943, according to the British report, many West Indians suffered loss of property and employment. One day in 1941 when the British minister commented to President Arias that with his new constitution tens of thousands of children of West Indians would be denied citizenship in his country, Arnulfo simply replied: "At any rate, I will not do as the Nazis do: I will not shoot them[8]." And his minister of government, Ricardo Adolfo de la Guardia, further elaborated: "We could not allow a black, English- speaking person to be elected president. The Panamanians are anxious to guard against the dangers that Panama, situated at the crossroads of the world, should degenerate from a Spanish-speaking "white" nation to a cosmopolitan congeries, a Babel of tongues, an utterly bastardized race[9]." The new constitution and laws prompted racist demonstrations by bigoted Panamanians, and worsened relations between the West Indian immigrants and Panamanians and made integration in Panama more difficult. During Arnulfo's brief time in office adults and senior West Indians grew frantic going to night school to learn Spanish overnight in order to satisfy the Arnulfo government's requirements to acquire legal status, and to obtain legitimate papers, whether to travel or to do business or even to reside in the country, and they were afraid of the daily anti-West Indian threats and rhetoric coming down from the anti-West Indian regime.

Arnulfo Arias, thankfully, was overthrown on October 10, 1941, twelve months after taking office and his first, second, and third vice presidents, Jose Pezet Arosemena, Ernesto Jaen Guardia and Anibal Rios Delgado, respectively were forced to resign. Ricardo Adolfo de La Guardia, Minister of Government and Justice, was complicit in the coup d'etat and the National Constituent Assembly appointed him to take Arnulfo Arias' place with the blessing of the American government, who backed the coup, for they were at war with Germany, and they hated Arnulfo Arias. Serving from October 1941 to June 1945, Ricardo De la Guardia gave more bases and concessions away to the American government than any other president, and he hated West Indians more than Arnulfo did. De la Guardia claimed that West Indians were overrunning his country, they were sub-humans who reproduced twice a year and he refused to authorize any more West Indian recruitment, insisting that those already in Panama should be confined to the Canal Zone and be repatriated back to the West Indies. Moreover, he told President Franklin Roosevelt he didn't want any black American soldiers operating in Panama and no more "niggers" should be brought to Panama[9].

That period of cruel and unjust treatment of West Indians by the Panamanian government fortunately did not last, thanks to the efforts of Francisco Arias Paredes (Don Pancho, who was head of the new liberal party and would have become Panama's next president in 1946 if he hadn't suddenly died in 1945 of a heart attack), and the National Civic League of Panamanians[10] that included leaders such as George Westerman, Sydney Young, Pedro N. Rhodes, as well as other influential Panamanian statesmen like Ricardo Alfaro, Harmodio Arias, Gil Blas Tejeira and his daughter Otilia, Juan D. Moscote, Felipe J. Escobar and others. They compiled thousands of signatures and petitioned the government to restore citizenship rights to West Indians born in Panama. Ricardo De la Guardia was forced to abrogate the 1941 Arnulfo Arias constitution in 1944 and his career ended in disgrace when he was removed by the newly formed National Constituent Assembly in 1945 and replaced by Enrique Adolfo Jimenez.

In 1946 a new constitution was adopted, replacing Arnulfo's that had for four years relegated first- and second- generation Panamanian West Indians to alien status in the country in which they were born. The new constitution restored their full rights as native born Panamanians and eased requirements for others to acquire citizenship. West Indians were happy because many of them who lived in Panama or who lived in the Canal Zone and had to do business in Panama, or were planning to live in Panama and did not have Panamanian citizenship papers, could remember those frightening and terrible days during Arnulfo's and De la Guardia's terms when West Indians were afraid to even venture across the border into Panamanian territory. World War II came to an end in 1945 with the demise of Hitler and the defeat of the Axis Alliance (Germany, Japan, and Italy) and after 1946 things seemed to improve for a little while for West Indians.

In May 1944 James Edwards had reached his 16th birthday when he completed the 9th grade which was added to the colored school curriculum just a few years earlier in 1941. Now, there were no more prospects of higher education for children of silver employees after the 9th grade, unless, as some of them did, they managed to enroll into overcrowded Spanish public schools in Panama. In the Edwards home it was decided that unless James got a job, he had to continue his public schooling in Panama. Many parents did not consider, however, how different the two school systems were and how difficult it was to place a young teenager like James from the Canal Zone public schools into his equivalent class in the Panama schools. First, he could not speak Spanish at all, living in the Canal Zone and growing up in the American culture and educational system from birth. Second, Panamanian educators seemed to have a bias against such transfers that, under proper pedagogical conditions and standards, should require an educational transcript evaluation, followed by an appropriate academic assessment and placement, taking language as only one of several factors into consideration. Unfortunately, in all cases, the only thing they used to evaluate transfers from the Canal Zone, was the Spanish language, consequently, James Edwards was placed in an elementary school classroom (in Escuela de Haiti, Parque LeFevre), setting him back academically by about 6 grade equivalents. He made the effort to attend the classes for about two months, but the barrier and the embarrassment were too much – especially when he had to sit in a classroom with little desks and little children who, compared to him, were too juvenile and intellectually immature to relate to. He couldn't continue. Fortunately for him, though, upon graduating from La Boca Jr. High he had sat for a competitive scholastic examination in English to see if he qualified for the La Boca Normal School teacher-training program that was being offered to West Indian youth in the Canal Zone who had just graduated from the 9th grade. At the same time when he decided to discontinue the failed Spanish school experiment, a letter came to his parents' home notifying him that he was selected as a successful normal school candidate.

The La Boca Normal Training School was established in 1935 to fill the shortage for qualified colored teachers to serve the growing Canal Zone colored school population. The elementary and junior high colored schools at that time were structured based on the American educational system, the same as the white schools, except that the colored schools were limited to second-hand quality facilities, books, materials, equipment, and fewer or no opportunities for advancement beyond the 7th grade junior high school level. Canal Zone authorities saw the La Boca Normal school as a simple and a convenient solution to the growing teacher shortage problem in the colored schools, and in fact, to them it was a cost-saving one; but they greatly underestimated its potential for developing a very high-quality teacher and leadership core in the Canal Zone silver communities. Thanks to the wisdom of Alfred E. Osborne[11] and his dedicated staff (a small cadre of experienced West Indian educators), a very competitive scholastic aptitude exam in English was selected and administered to the brightest junior high school graduates in all the silver towns in the Canal Zone -- Silver City and Gatun on the Atlantic side and Gamboa, Paraiso, Red Tank, and La Boca on the Pacific side -- and they recruited the top candidates to participate in a rigorous training program that consisted of 3 years of senior high school courses and

4 years of college courses combined and compressed into a total of 4 years while still meeting the highest possible academic standards. In fact, unsuspecting to the Canal Zone authorities, Alfred E. Osborne was developing future leaders of the Black community.[12&13] James' family was very happy when he was selected as one of the top 25 successful candidates out of hundreds of applicants who took the exam and were accepted into the third Normal School class starting in the year, 1944; therefore, they made sure he enrolled and doted on him and encouraged him every day.

He was the youngest in his family and no one else had gone that far in school. The situation at home was critical, though, because his parents were trying very hard to save every penny in order to build a modest retirement home in Parque Lefevre, a suburb of Panama City where they were going to live when his father was superannuated -- laid off without a real pension but with a small monthly disability relief payment -- and they would have to vacate the Canal Zone quarters and move into Panama or repatriate back to the West Indies.

At the age of 65, West Indian workers were terminated and given a disability relief dispensation of 0$ to $25/mo. depending on how many years they had served (a dollar for each year up to 25 years), how much money they saved in the bank, how much furniture they had, how much property they owned, etc.[14&15] which could reduce the payment to zero in some cases, as in the case of Mr. Peter Samuel Martin who, unfortunately, had saved up $10,000 (a miracle by itself) after a lifetime of very frugal living over the 40-50 years he worked for the Panama Canal Zone government and, therefore, he got zero disability relief.

Mr. Edwards' salary was hardly enough to take care of his family and afford additional expenses for he had very little disposable income, so his wife, Marie, like many West Indian wives in those days, helped out by taking in bachelors' and white people's clothes to wash and iron in order to supplement the family income. (Some West Indian women also served as housemaids and servants to white families to earn extra income). They had decided that since James was accepted when he applied to that new school, they were going to help him no matter what sacrifices they had to make.

"Son," his mother said to him, "I want you to finish that school and have a profession and find a nice, single young lady without blemish to marry and give your father and me grandchildren before we pass away."

And his dad also encouraged him.

"Make us proud, son, you know your mother and I never went further than the 4th grade, so make us proud."

Thank Heaven he had a sister, Ivy, who had a sales assistant job in the commissary and quite often she pitched in and took up the slack to help. His three other siblings, two older brothers and another sister, were struggling to make it on their own and were not able to support him. He and big sis were tight. Although he never liked to go to her whenever he needed financial help, she made it hard for him not to depend on her, she kept in touch with him constantly, wanting to know everything about his schedule, his needs, his school expenses, planned trips, even his meals and incidentals. He was glad to know that in his elder sister he had a second mother to help him during his normal school years. When she got married and moved to Panama City and was living in the Omphroy building on Central Avenue, you couldn't keep him away during the carnival season. From her balcony, she had a great view of the parade. He remembers the 1947 Carnival like it was yesterday.

"Sis," he said to her, "you have the best spot to see the parade, do you realize that?"

"Yes, we do, and the rest of the balcony is filling up fast. The parade is starting from Sabanas and coming this way down Central Avenue in about a half hour from now.”

He was lucky his sister and her husband lived on the 2nd floor of the Omphroy building overlooking Central Avenue and their corner apartment opened onto the balcony. You could see everything that went by from there. Facing them was the Muller building on the opposite side of Central Avenue.

“Sis, I am glad we are not over there on the Muller building balcony, it’s not as secure as your building which is made of concrete. Remember what happened 2 years ago during the parade when the third-floor balcony collapsed. Children were hanging for dear life from the iron connecting bars on the balcony where they had perched. I don’t know how comes nobody got killed, but a lot of people, they say, were badly injured. Don’t you remember?”

“Of course, I remember, and they fixed the balcony and made it stronger and safer. Since then they also set a limit on the number of people who can go onto that balcony. People can’t just go up there off the street anymore unless they live there or are accounted for by the people who live there. They’re not going to let that happen again, believe me.”

“I hope so. Anyway, you still won’t find me on that balcony any time soon.”

By then the parade was in high gear as it approached, and everyone's neck grew a few more inches to get a good view. There were all kinds of disfrazes, devils and demons in the street, comparsas, bands, beautiful polleras in open cars, men dressed in handsome montunos, trucks with dancers, numerous floats representing different organizations including floats from the "Zonians," and, best of all, there was the most gorgeous, the most bedecked float of all, the float of the official queen of the carnival and her royal court surrounding her, followed by a few lesser floats and a number of street walkers and dancers in costumes. Many demonios (devils) marching in the street were local people who worked hard all year making devil masks and sewing their devil costumes to claim prizes for the best devil costumes in that year's parade. It was a most beautiful parade. Meanwhile, James and his family and friends ate and drank their fill while they sat and took it all in from their balcony perches. And when it was over the party didn't stop there. People kept partying and carousing all night long in toldos, clubs, bars, homes, and in the streets driving away demons and evil spirits before the Lenten season began the next day, Ash Wednesday. The next day there was a massive cleanup in the streets along the parade route and people tried their best to resume their everyday lives until next year's carnival came around.

"Well, did you have a good time?" his sister asked him the following day when they spoke.

"I sure did," he admitted to her. "Now it's back to school and the completion of the second half of my junior year."

James' junior and senior years in the Normal School coincided with the term in office of the new Panamanian President after the war, Enrique Adolfo Jimenez (1945-1948). President Jimenez had signed into law the new 1946 constitution and, unlike his two anti-West Indian predecessors, defended West Indian rights as Panamanian citizens in the Republic and their rights as Panamanian workers on the Canal Zone to claim equal opportunity and equal treatment by the U. S., as called for in the 1936 Hull-Alfaro treaty and as stipulated in the U.S. Secretary of State Cordell Hull's note regarding "fair employment practices and equal employment opportunities between U. S. and Panamanian citizens.[16]" President Jimenez' action was very helpful in supporting Local 713 in its negotiations with Canal Zone authorities and this enabled the union to unify Panamanians of West Indian origin and Hispanics who worked in the Canal Zone.

In addition to supporting the West Indian cause as the sitting president, Enrique A. Jimenez was responsible for the construction of the Tocumen

International Airport in 1947; for creating the Colon Free Trade Zone with Law No. 18 on June 17, 1948; for establishing the Felix Olivares School in Chiriqui province and the Abel Bravo School in Colon; signing legislation that supported education and university autonomy; and promoting the development of University City and the development of Hotel El Panama during his term in Office. (He was later honored posthumously by Panama when they named after him, in 2013, the "Enrique Adolfo Jimenez International Airport" in Colon.)

For a while, then, in the late 1940's, it appeared that the conditions for a better quality of life for West Indians in the Panama Canal Zone were improving somewhat: (1) The Jimenez administration was supportive of the West Indian cause; (2) on the world scene the nemesis of Adolf Hitler and the devastating WWII were over; (3) Harry S. Truman, the 33rd president of the United States (1945-1953), issued Executive Order 9981 in 1948 which abolished segregation in the Armed Forces; (4) during the successive governorships in the Canal Zone of Joseph C. Mehaffey ('44-'48), Frances K. Newcomer ('48-'52), and John Seybold ('52-'56) the strongest voices and resistance among first generation (criollos) and second generation West Indians rose up against the oppressive racist system that existed on the Canal

Zone and the pressure for change was mounting from all sides.

The Association of Colored School Teachers which was led by normal school graduates, and which was the precursor to the strong Local 713 Labor Union, had been petitioning the Canal Zone government since the early 1940's for higher education opportunities for West Indian youth in the Canal Zone. Joining with other community leaders they pressed the struggle into the mid-1940's gaining an important ally in the Canal Zone, Lawrence Johnson[17], Director of Colored Schools (1935-36), Assistant Superintendent of Canal Zone Schools (1936-47), Superintendent of Canal Zone Schools (1948-1953). He was a liberal-minded white official in the Canal Zone School System who worked with leaders in the Black community to upgrade the so-called colored schools, notwithstanding racially discriminatory policies and practices of the segregationists who ran the Panama Canal Zone and who wished to provide West Indians with minimal education limited only to a bare literacy and servitude level. (*It is said that he later paid a high price for his efforts in helping to improve education in the black community.)

During Johnson's tenure[18] as Director of Colored Schools, in 1935, the La Boca Normal Training School was established; as Assistant Superintendent he was instrumental in adding the 9th grade to the curriculum in 1941; as Superintendent of the Canal Zone Schools in 1948 a Summer Institute was established to help "silver" teachers upgrade their skills and acquire accreditation to secure professional advancement; also, "colored" teachers were encouraged by him to go abroad and obtain advanced degrees and on their return Johnson promoted them to U.S. pay scales based on those credentials (1948-52); and, finally, while serving as Assistant then Superintendent of C. Z. schools, Johnson was responsible for designing, creating and establishing the La Boca and Silver City Vocational High Schools in 1946 and 1949 respectively, and for establishing the La Boca branch of the Canal Zone Junior College in 1950. West Indian students in the Atlantic side towns would commute by bus to Silver City Occupational High School and those living in the Pacific side towns would commute to La Boca Occupational High School. The collaboration between West Indian educators and Superintendent Lawrence Johnson in building up the colored schools served as a vehicle by which Johnson was able to obtain his PhD. degree in 1949 from Stanford University, California. The thesis of his dissertation was: **"The Upward Extension of the Canal Zone Schools for Native Colored Children."**

Alfred E. Osborne[19], a graduate of both Chicago and Columbia Universities and the son of David Osborne (a West Indian pioneer schoolteacher and principal in the construction era Canal Zone colored schools, as well as an ordained Episcopal minister) was appointed through Johnson as the Supervisor of Colored Schools in 1939 after he had served as the first principal of the La Boca Normal School (1935-38).

Osborne was an apostle of the New School Movement he had studied while attending Chicago and Columbia Universities and, based on its principles, in 1938 he, along with Leonor Jump and Peter Samuel Martin, wrote a curriculum guide[20]: "General Objectives of the Canal Zone Colored Schools" which served to educate all new teachers in the La Boca Normal Training School and which became the guide for teaching in the colored schools after 1938. It focused on **"student-centered learning wherein the student should be encouraged to seek out knowledge for personal growth; they should be awakened to the world around them (as world citizens) and should be given tools to understand it on their own terms. Their personalities, skills, and ambitions should all interact with the environment to guide them into adulthood. Schools should inspire students to bring into the classroom as broad a spectrum as possible of life experiences.**

Everyone should experiment with music, art, carpentry, literature, language, science, and social studies to develop preferences. Avocations shape personality just as much as vocations and play a positive role in learning, therefore the guide also stressed leisure activities and sports as constructive pastimes to promote growth and development after formal schooling ended."

Contrary to the intent of racist Canal Zone officials, Osborne turned the "colored" school classrooms into laboratories for studying democracy, science, literature, and the world at large. Mr. Osborne's collaboration with Lawrence Johnson was the ideal partnership that the West Indian communities needed; they were both dedicated to the improvement of education for West Indians in the Canal Zone.

Beside improvements in education achieved during the decade of the 1940's, in the years 1942-1946 the Isthmian Negro Youth Congress (INYC), a youth movement that was created by inspired community leaders and educators such as Sidney A. Young, editor of the Panama Tribune, George Westerman, statesman and promoter, Alfred E. Osborne, administrator of colored schools, Aston M. Parchment, teacher and athletics director, and several other community activists, served as a forum for self-improvement of the West Indian youth in the Panama Canal Zone and helped to turn them away from idleness and delinquent behavior toward focusing on self-improvement. The INYC strove to instill a spirit of pride in African American history, in the youth themselves and in their communities. They published a quarterly bulletin that contained articles, essays, poetry, and information of public interest to the black communities; they actively conducted programs and civic and social activities in the West Indian communities with emphasis on "Progress through Education" to encourage and motivate the growing youth population; and they even talked about the right to United States citizenship for West Indians born in the Canal Zone. (Since the Canal Zone lifestyle and culture at that time was 100% U. S. oriented and Americans claimed that the Canal Zone was U.S. territory.) The INYC also motivated and helped to prepare many of these same youngsters to take advantage of the opportunity when the doors of the new vocational high schools in La Boca and Silver City, Canal Zone opened for colored students in 1946 and 1949 respectively.

In another critical area, the area of labor relations for West Indian workers on the Canal Zone, for the first time since the failed 1920 labor strike when "silver" workers were severely penalized and barred from unionizing, and, after the demise of the Panama Canal West Indian Employees Association (PCWIEA) under its President, Samuel H. Whyte, that from 1926-1945 represented West Indian workers while being barred from striking, engaging in any kind of work stoppage or organizing activities and being reduced to what amounted only to pleas and appeals with no teeth or bargaining power against a local government that had a non-existent sense of fairness and generosity toward black workers, beginning in 1945 Local 713 labor union replaced the PCWIEA and successfully gained recognition and approval by the top U.S. Military brass Henry L. Stimson, U.S. Secretary of War, as the official silver workers bargaining unit led by Edward Gaskin[21] who was a graduate of the first Normal School class, the class of 1938, and who, in 1946, became the Principal of La Boca Elementary and Junior High School. This was in the early stage of Gaskin becoming a powerful champion for change in the epic struggle against racism in the Canal Zone. Gaskin would engage the local Canal Zone power structure relentlessly with grievances (at the risk of retaliation against him by the white government who did everything they could to ruin him – especially after he (like George Westerman) in 1947 and 1948 travelled to the U.S. and rallied U.S. anti-discrimination forces against the Canal Zone government's racism and mistreatment of

West Indians. He stood his ground in labor negotiations and would later exert a strong influence and play a significant role in the mass protests and rallies leading up to the negotiations that resulted in the U.S.-Panama Remon-Eisenhower Treaty of 1955. Also, through Local 713's ties with the U. S. parent organization, the UPWA and its Secretary-Treasurer Ewart Guinier[22] (a Panamanian West Indian born in Panama in 1910 and emigrated to the U.S. in 1925), Gaskin and local union leaders were able to influence the esteemed singer and activist Paul Robeson, who already had strong ties to the labor movement in the U.S. and to anti-discrimination causes, to come to the Isthmus of Panama and give a series of concerts both in the Colon Arena and in the Panama National Stadium. Robeson refused to sing in the Canal Zone to white people, no matter what they offered him[23]. "I never have and never will sing in places where my people are segregated in the audience", said Robeson. The Canal Zone government, in turn, boycotted him but the Panamanian government under President Enrique Adolfo Jimenez welcomed Robeson with open arms, turned out in full force to attend his concerts and escorted him on municipal tours. Many whites from the Canal Zone went into Colon and Panama to hear him sing at the Colon Arena and the Panama National Stadium.

On May 28, 1947, during his very busy concert schedule, Paul Robeson, one of the most famous artists of his time, while on tour in Panama visited the La Boca Normal Training School to speak to students and teachers. As preparations were being made the day before his visit you could hear in the hallway the excitement of a group of normal school students who were to graduate as the classes of '47, '48 and '49.

"You think we'll have enough room in the library tomorrow? Everybody is going to be there. There are only about 75-100 seats," said one student.

"That's why we tried to keep it quiet, if at all possible, and limited the number of invitations," said another.

"Our director had arranged a special visit for our classes only," said a third student, "Mr. Robeson is going to be here for just a short visit only and then they're going to whisk him off to get ready for the big open-air concert in the national stadium. I don't even think he's going to have time to sing for us; he's just going to say a few words and that's it."

"Even so, I can't wait to meet him and shake his hand," said a fourth, "He's a great man."

"Of course, he is! He's Paul Robeson, the greatest baritone who ever lived and a fighter for justice and equal rights," said a fifth student.

"Just make sure I get a good seat tomorrow," said the first student addressing another who was on the planning committee.

"Just make sure you're there early," was the response, "It's going to be first come first served."

The next day at 11 a.m. the La Boca School library -- with its walls decorated with 50 large autographed framed portraits of famous black American heroes and its bookshelves stacked with a thousand books on black history (all contributed through the efforts of George Westerman and Leonor Jump, members of the La Boca library committee) -- was crowded to capacity. Not a seat was vacant as people stood in the hallway.

Paul Robeson entered the room, accompanied by the officials of the La Boca Normal School and the head of Local 713 who sponsored him, and stood in the front of the library, a tall, muscular, very confident, giant of a man, and, after an introduction, followed by a rousing welcoming applause, he spoke. His deep baritone voice reverberated in every ear in the room and hallway as he greeted the students and faculty warmly and encouraged them to continue the fight here on the Canal Zone for equal justice and better conditions for Black people. He thanked their leaders for inviting him to come and speak to the class and encouraged them as students to study hard and to dedicate themselves to uplifting their race, for them to do their part as he is doing his with all his might and talent in the struggle for freedom and equality. As much as his words were uplifting, the students were dying for a song, and he could not help but oblige them. The room vibrated with his deep bass voice as they absorbed every note of the folk songs "Oh no, John" and "Let My People Go" that resonated through their bodies and souls. Afterwards they gave him a resounding applause and thanked him, and they hated to see him leave.

Two years after Robeson's visit, "Westerman Concerts" was officially launched and it brought to the Isthmus other outstanding African American artists and world famous African American icons to perform on the concert stage. Some of these famous artists were Emily Butcher (classical pianist), Dorothy Maynor (singer), Phyllipa Schulyer (classical pianist), Hazel Scott (jazz pianist), Todd Duncan (light baritone), William Warfield (baritone), and the greatest contralto voice in the universe, Marian Anderson who gave concerts in the Panama National Theatre in 1951. James Edwards was so moved by her singing that he attended her concerts three times and each time fought back tears of joy. What an inspiration it was to West Indian youths who were fortunate enough to hear and meet these famous icons of the concert stage and famous African American heroes.

The decade of 1940-1950, therefore, although in the beginning seemed discouraging, turned out to be a most productive and exciting time and reached its peak when West Indians began making progress educationally, professionally, and politically in the Canal Zone and in Panama, and, for a brief cosmic moment seemed to be on their way to achieving still greater progress. During the latter part of the decade, when that glimmer of hope and promise were awakened, young teacher candidates of the class of 1948 were highly motivated and could hardly wait to complete their training and begin their teaching careers.

One week after Paul Robeson's visit, the Normal School recessed for a 2-month summer vacation (June - July 1947). The class of '47 graduated that June and the other two classes, the 48ers and 49ers, returned home to relax though some engaged in part-time employment during the summer. When these continuing students returned from their summer vacations, they resumed their studies of teaching methods and strategies in the subject areas (reading, arithmetic, social studies, and science), and the study of classroom organization and management. Beside teaching strategies, their four-year development included character building and leadership skills training and to apply what they learned in these two areas of development throughout the four years they engaged in activities such as school plays, academic debates, running a student association, publishing a newspaper (the Gasp), participating in sports, luncheons, buffet suppers, talent shows, nights of fun, informal and formal dances, and outings and trips to the interior which helped to enrich their lives and memorialize their school experiences in their minds and hearts for years to come.

Music was such a significant part of the four-year curriculum that in addition to being trained to teach music to elementary and junior high school children, as members of the La Boca Normal School glee club they engaged in weekly practice which engendered in them enjoyment and love for music. With this experience they looked forward to giving many concert performances under the excellent music directorship of Ms. Emily Butcher, a first-generation Panamanian-West Indian native of La Boca, Panama Canal Zone, an accomplished concert pianist, and a gifted music director who graduated from the first normal school class, from the Panama National Conservatory of Music, and from Teachers College, Columbia University. When December 1947 came, signaling the approaching end of four years of academic preparation and scholarship for the class of '48, it also represented the fulfillment of many hours of rehearsals and performances that brought the art of choral singing to new heights in Panama, thanks to the La Boca Normal School Glee Club Ensemble conducted by its distinguished music director. They gave benefit concerts at festivities, on special occasions in concert halls and public venues, including hospitals, and one memorable trip to the Leper Colony at Palo Seco, a few miles across the ferry, where they performed to the delight of residents and staff. To close out the Christmas season, in their most harmonious voices the glee club achieved its apotheosis with a brilliant Christmas concert in the La Boca School auditorium featuring songs from Handel's Messiah, spirituals and other holiday classics. A day or two later to finally bring the calendar year to a close as the holiday season advanced, a small group of singers went caroling through the streets of La Boca town to the delight of residents.

January, 1948 came and with it the beginning of the cadetship program that provided an opportunity to put into practice what they had learned in their classroom laboratories. With the help and guidance of dedicated and experienced teachers, with a dedicated principal, Leonor Jump, and an enlightened supervisor of instruction, Alfred E. Osborne, a staunch advocate of the New School philosophy of education theories of learning and progressive methodology and principles of teaching, Normal School graduates were shaped into excellent educators. They were the proud home-grown children and grandchildren of the so-called "silver" people whose ancestors were shipped from Africa in slave ships to labor in the Caribbean fields, and, after becoming freed men, transported as cheap labor to the jungles of Panama to dig the now famous Panama Canal.

Panama Canal Zone West Indian youth, descendants of the "silver people," were therefore fortunate to have been molded in the Canal Zone elementary and junior high schools by (a) educators who graduated from many of the finest Caribbean colleges (such as Mico College, St. George College, St. Joseph's College, Shortwood, etc.) who were pioneers[24] in the early Canal Zone colored schools, and by (b) first generation teachers (criollos) who received their elementary, junior high and normal school training in the Canal Zone colored schools under aforementioned pioneer educators. Some of these "criollos" went on to graduate from U.S. colleges and/or from professional institutions in the Republic of Panama.

All West Indian youths who graduated from Canal Zone schools were beneficiaries of educators who came before them and who laid for them a sound foundation to grow from and be proud of. West Indian educators were all determined to pass on their knowledge and wisdom and to provide the best education possible to their succeeding generations despite social and economic limitations in what was originally intended by the local power structure to be an inferior, racially segregated, and biased colored Canal Zone school system limited to elementary and junior high school level training up to the 7th grade and later the 8th grade.

As the last school year ended for the fourth La Boca Normal School class, the class of '48, the atmosphere was abuzz with excitement and expectations and before long the final school break of Easter 1948 had arrived. That Easter Sunday, March 28, 1948, after the St. Theresa church service ended, James Edwards returned home from attending mass and later that evening joined his family for Easter dinner, the last one they would share together at their old address in La Boca, C.Z. because by the next Easter of 1949 pop would be retired (superannuated) and mom and pop would be living in their new home built by the help and hands of friends and fellow West Indian craftsmen in a section called Parque Lefevre in the suburbs of Panama City. That Sunday was also the last day on earth for Chanticleer, that healthy, vociferous rooster who would crow no more from his kitchen room perch where they kept him until the master chef, James' mom, was ready to cook him and another fat hen for Easter when she prepared the most delectable chicken dinner. Yes, James had a lot to be thankful for.

"When is your graduation from the Normal School taking place?" asked one of his brothers during dinner.

"June 6th, two months and a few days from today," he responded, "I can't wait to finish and start teaching."

"I can't wait to see you graduate either, and neither can mom and dad for you know how much they have sacrificed," said sis who had come with her husband Bertrand Martin to join the family for Easter dinner.

"Yes, and you, too, sis," said James, "If it weren't for you I could never have made it. Just two months left and it will be over. And you'll be looking at the first schoolteacher in this family."

The help from his elder sister while his parents were busy building their retirement home in Parque Lefevre was a Godsend. She virtually supported him for four years with all of his expenses.

Before they realized it the last two months, which were the busiest of the school year, came with final reports due, final evaluations, yearbook assignments, planning for the final black and white graduation ball at the Panama Hilton hotel and the graduation exercise on the last day, June 6, 1948. Suddenly it was the end of their schooling and James and his classmates were thrilled for having completed the four years of intensive teacher training (now that their senior year had come to its close) mixed with the excitement of knowing that for them a new and more challenging phase of life was about to begin.

Chapter V:

Silver City, C.Z., Life Away from Home

There were 23 out of 24 candidates who graduated in the class of '48. After returning home to their respective Canal Zone silver towns for a two-month summer hiatus, they reported to their assigned schools to begin their teaching assignments. James and four other classmates were assigned to Silver City elementary school to fill vacancies there and the other 18 graduates were distributed among the remaining five silver towns: Gatun, Gamboa [Sta. Cruz], Paraiso, Red Tank, and La Boca. From the night before leaving home his mother made sure that his luggage and bags were packed not only with his clothes but also with nice treats she cooked and a cake she baked for him so he would not forget mom's good food and would miss her when he was away. As heavy as these items made his load, within two or three days after arriving in Colon he wasted no time vanquishing all the good treats she had carefully packed. Of course, every Friday evening he was on the train bound for Panama City heading home to renew his acquaintance with her cooking and baking. He was assigned quarters in a bachelor compound in Mt. Hope near the printing plant which was not very far from

Silver City Elementary School, although he usually took a bus from the bus stop there into Silver City.

Silver City was another segregated non-white civilian town that was part of the U.S. occupied Canal Zone south of the city of Colon. In the 40's and early 50's it developed into one of the most populated silver towns in the canal zone on the Atlantic side with more than 50% of it consisting of children of West Indians and other non-U.S. workers. Like most silver communities during that time, it was made up mostly of immigrant Panama Canal workers from Caribbean countries with a wide range of skills including maintenance workers, sanitation workers, janitors, dock workers, boiler workers, chauffeurs, butchers, cooks, carpenters, electricians, blacksmiths, plumbers, painters, riveters, drillers, masons, metal workers, truck drivers, truck repairmen, railroad workers, checkers, timekeepers, clerks, office helpers, preachers, schoolteachers, and like most silver communities it's streets bore West Indian names like Jamaica St., Barbados St., Trinidad St., Grenada St., Martinique St., Saint Lucia St, except for Randolph Rd., since Randolph is not a West Indian name, but an American army officer for whom the street was originally named when it was part of a U. S. military installation before being made a part of the town of Silver City. Silver City and adjacent silver towns would grow as they expanded until they surpassed the combined white populations of Margarita, Cristobal, and Coco Solo. The need for elementary education was indeed great and the mission of "colored" teachers like James and his colleagues was extremely vital. They had no trouble filling Silver City Elementary School classrooms with students.

James reported a few days before classes began and attended a staff meeting on Thursday, July 29, 1948, in which he met the principal and other staff members. In that first meeting, William Weakley, principal, a short stocky bundle of energy, who is not known for his public speaking ability, addressed the staff.

"Good morning, my name is Principal Weakley. I am glad to see our regular teachers who are back from summer vacation, and to see that we have some new faces among us as well. Before we start, will each of the new teachers please stand and introduce yourselves at this time so that we can all get to know each other better."

This took only a few minutes and afterwards Weakley resumed his little speech.

"Now that we have taken care of the introductions, I officially welcome you all to Silver

City Elementary School, one of the largest colored schools in the Canal Zone. I look forward to us having a very successful school year together. I am not one who likes to talk too much; therefore, for fear of talking too much and saying too little, I now turn the meeting over to my able assistant, Wilmer Mathewson, who will go over with you all the necessary details to get you started. My office is always open to you if you have any questions. Again, I welcome you, especially the new teachers, and wish you all the best school year possible."

With those brief remarks Weakley excused himself from the meeting and Wilmer Mathewson, a graduate of the normal school class of '47, proceeded to distribute keys, school calendars, class schedules and assignment changes if any. The veteran teachers were familiar with the procedures, had always worked well with Principal Weakley, did not have any problems and were eager to leave the meeting to begin preparations for their classes, so Wilmer dismissed them and only the new teachers remained who included Darryl Anders, Rudolph Barnes, Ronald Wilson, Daisy Biggett, and James Edwards. He went over all of the procedures, schedules, calendar and assignments that were new to them and answered any questions.

"Since you will be teaching third through sixth grade students," said Wilmer, "make sure you get the correct level reading, arithmetic, social studies, and science textbooks for your classes. Either pick them up from the storeroom or arrange to have the storeroom clerk deliver them to your respective classrooms. Make sure you count them and you have enough for your students. You'll be responsible if any books issued to you are missing. Also, pick up the supplies you need such as writing pads, pens, chalk, paper, erasures, etc. You have closets in your classrooms where you will store your books and supplies. Don't be bothering me or the storeroom clerk after today for supplies unless it is an emergency. Brief lesson outlines must be written on the blackboards and written lesson plans must be available when requested. Are there any questions?" After a brief pause... "Good. Principal Weakley will be stopping in from time to time to see how you are doing, good luck."

They returned to their classrooms to finish preparations and have their books and supplies checked and put away in classroom closets. What was not finished was completed the next day, Friday, July 30, 1948.

On Monday morning, August 2, 1948, the first day of classes, James was greeted by 28 impressionable

3rd and 4th grade students eager to learn. He was assigned a split-level grade, half of them 3rd graders and half 4th graders in one classroom. With a split-level class each grade would occupy half of the room and have a different level reading, math, and science book. Their lessons would alternate. While one grade is silently studying the other would be engaged by the teacher in directed reading, class discussion or lesson review; then they would be given an assignment and the teacher would rotate to the other half of the room and vice versa. In certain lessons like music, art, and penmanship the entire body would participate together. He accepted the challenge and enjoyed the experience and would come to know his students and their parents very well during that school year and would appreciate the Caribbean population's love and respect for education and their dedication to instilling that love in their children. It was an ideal teaching environment where discipline was concerned, for there were few or no disciplinary problems, which motivated and enabled him to devote his teaching ability to raising his students' reading and math levels, awareness of science, knowledge of the world around them, and their love of music for that became a most enjoyable part of the daily curriculum. He loved to teach them music by sight reading after he taught them solfeo and a one-octave vocal scale with the help of a pitch pipe which was the foundation for learning to sight read and sing simple tunes and rounds acapella by notes which they enjoyed singing so much that after the music class was over, even on hot days, the rest of the afternoon went well and was very satisfying due to the effect that music had on his students. By the end of the first year, he realized how much he loved teaching and how much he had inspired and was inspired by his first class of 3rd and 4th graders.

In his second school year, August 1949 to May 1950, he was assigned a straight 4th grade with some of his previous third graders who were promoted and some new students added. By the end of that second year, he and his colleagues were better known and were respected by the community. In fact, being a teacher in the Caribbean community was a highly regarded and respected profession. If you were a schoolteacher, wherever you went in the town you were looked up to and greeted with respect. But even though he had been there two years already he hadn't really gotten to know many people on a personal basis, probably out of his shyness and being reserved, or perhaps because during his first two years he was more eager to catch the Friday evening train to go back home on weekends to fulfill family and personal commitments. Anyway, his closest friends in Colon were mostly his co-workers, and other normal school graduates who like him were teaching in the elementary or in the junior high school of Silver City, C. Z. One of those friends was Harvey Corbin, a normal school graduate of the class of '47 and a resident of Colon and member of a large, well-known family in both Colon and Silver City social circles, and, as his best friend, Harvey would henceforth make certain that James got to know his relatives and friends in Silver City and Colon quite well.

Silver City Jr. High was only a short walk from the elementary school and of the class of '48 only Lon Carswell was assigned there to teach in the social studies department. Harvey, who also taught English in the junior high school, came by often to see Principal Weakley about some administrative matter, and, one afternoon two months into the 1950-51 schoolyear, he stopped by James' classroom just after he had dismissed his students and Harvey peeked in through the doorway.

"Hi, James, what are you doing this evening?"

"Just some papers I must grade. Otherwise, not much I suppose."

"You know, Jim, life is more than just about teaching. You must relax, too, get around and socialize a bit. You've been working here two school years already and from what I can tell you don't seem

90

to be getting around much since you've been here. You must start getting to know people or they will think something is wrong with you. I know what. Come with me, I am meeting some friends in Colon in about an hour and I'd like to introduce you to them."

He could not resist Harvey's laissez-faire, bon vivant spirit and it came when his social life in this town away from home needed a little boost.

Okay, let me put away a few things. Tomorrow is Friday anyway and I'll be able to catch up."

And off they went into Colon with Harvey leading the way. First, they stopped by a shoe repair shop to drop off a pair of shoes for Harvey's girlfriend, then they passed by a popular local club where Harvey was planning to meet some friends and there James got his first real initiation into Colon social life.

"Hi Charlie," Harvey greeted the bartender who returned his greeting.

"Hi teach!"

It seemed like everybody in the bar recognized Harvey as they walked in. He had a way of standing out everywhere he went. He was a habitual smoker, there was always a cigarette in his mouth and he puffed it like it gave him so much pleasure just inhaling and jettisoning the smoke out without stopping; and don't let him run out of cigarettes, he'd go bumming anybody and everybody for a cigarette and he would die if he didn't get a replacement pack in a hurry. He had a nice Charlie Chaplain moustache and a couple of gold teeth in the front of his mouth, and he always had an aura like he was in some kind of urgency. Finally, he reached the table at the back of the room where his friends were seated.

"Hi fellows," said Harvey, "meet James, a good friend of mine; we went to school together and he is in his 3rd year teaching at the elementary school," and turning to James, "James, meet George, Andy, Rena, Roy, and Samuel."

"Hi, James," they said almost in unison.

"How do you like Colon so far?" asked Rena.

"Well, I haven't seen a whole lot of it even though I have been working here a while now; but I like the school and the town of Silver City very much."

"Don't worry," said Andy, Rena's boyfriend, "If I know Harvey, from now on you'll be seeing a lot more of it."

"Yeah, especially the risqué parts," added Roy.

And everyone began to laugh at Harvey's expense as he broke into a sheepish smile that he couldn't hide.

And from that moment James was initiated into his first Colon social circle, a let-your-hair-down, any-subject-allowed, uninhibited, friendly, jovial group that had a lot of local gossip to share with some spicy anecdotes and risqué jokes tossed in. This was a regular once-a-week meeting place. First, they chowed down some beef fried rice since most of them, like James, were hungry; then the drinks, multiple drinks, started flowing generously until after 3 drinks James had to turn the rest down.

"No more for me, please." He said to Harvey and his friends.

And they continued having a good time discussing local politics and social gossip until about 9:00 p.m. when James got up to leave. They tried to persuade him to stay a while longer, but he wouldn't. He thanked them for showing him a good time and said he looked forward to joining them again perhaps on a weekend, but tonight, Thursday, he had to call it a night. He told Harvey he would see him the next day and left to catch a bus to go home.

The next day when he ran into Harvey it didn't seem like the previous night had any effect on him at all, seeing as how he didn't get home until probably after midnight. He was alert as if lack of sleep doesn't bother him and he was ready for the weekend agenda. He invited James to come and meet some of his family and some more of his friends, but James had already planned to go home that Friday evening.

"If I had known ahead of time," said James, "I would have arranged to stay over, but my folks are expecting me. Let's make it next weekend. That way I'll let them know in advance."

"Okay," said Harvey, "until next Friday then."

And there, in Harvey Corbin he had found his best guide and contact for finally getting immersed in Colon society.

Chapter VI:

A Dose of Humor and Local History

The next Friday, September 29, 1950, after work, James met Harvey in Colon at the intersection of Melendez Avenue and 9th Street and they went nearby to the apartment of Harvey's sister-in-law, Marlene, and his elder brother, Lucas Corbin, who worked as a timekeeper on the Cristobal docks and who had asked Harvey to let James know that he was coming to dinner so he should not make any other arrangements. They got there about 6:15 p.m., a few minutes later than expected.

"Good evening sis and bro," said Harvey as they entered.

"Hi Harvey," said Marlene.

"Hi Harvey, so you finally got here; you must be very tired!" (A hint that he must have walked all the way) said his brother jokingly.

"Sorry about that," replied Harvey, "the buses were a little slow today. I'd like to introduce a good friend of mine from Normal School days. James, this is Marlene, my brother's beautiful wife and this here is my inimitable brother, Lucas or Luke for short. Marlene and Luke, this is James Edwards whom I told you about. He's from La Boca and he teaches at the Silver City Elementary School."

"Hello, James, welcome to our home," said Marlene.

"I am glad to meet you, James," said Lucas, "and don't be shy; make yourself at home."

After James and Harvey were comfortably seated Lucas served them both a drink and started to entertain them, which he was good at.

"By the way," said Lucas, "some people call me Lucas and some people call me Luke half of the time. You can use whichever one you prefer. The name means 'bringer of light, joy, laughter'. It's a Greek name; it's in the Bible somewhere."

"Oh, that's good to know," said James.

"Harvey tells me you play chess," Lucas said to James.

"Yes, I play a little."

"You know, I once had a monkey who loved to play chess," said Lucas.

"You're kidding me; you had a monkey who played chess? He must have been a very clever monkey."

"Not really," said Lucas, "whenever we played, I usually beat him two out of three games!"

"Yeah, and chickens have teeth and can talk!" said James. "Where is this monkey now?"

"He died," said Lucas "and I miss him already though not only because of chess, but because he was a very funny monkey."

"What was so funny about him?" asked James.

"One day I was telling him a joke and he laughed so hard he keeled over and died with a big grin on his face."

James still didn't laugh at Luke's corny joke and Luke was determined to get a laugh out of him yet. But he waited until after dinner during which Marlene had a chance to converse with him and asked him about his relatives and if he had any who lived in Colon or if he had any family anywhere on the Atlantic side.

"I heard my father mention once that he had a foster son who left La Boca as a young man and came to Colon to live, but he never kept track of him."

"What's the young man's name?" asked Marlene.

"The name I remember is Charlie Whyte, but I wouldn't know where to look for him."

And she turned to Luke and asked if he ever heard of that name, which Luke said he had not, but he would find out and get the information for her to give to Harvey's friend. The rest of the conversation during dinner was pleasant and afterwards they left the dinner table for the living room sofa. Luke was only too glad to serve some more drinks and to resume his effort to get James to laugh.

"Here, let's have some men-size drinks and talk some more," he said. "You ever heard about a place called 'Monkey Hill'?"

"Isn't that the same place they call Mount Hope Cemetery?" asked James.

"Yes," said Harvey anxious to contribute to the conversation, "from the French construction time they used to bury West Indians there."

"That place was the monkeys' home before they came there and started burying people there," added Luke. "I think the monkeys are trying to make a statement. Besides, they still have fruit trees in the area which monkeys like. They don't bother the dead and the dead don't bother them."

"I'm sure they don't," said James.

"By the way," said Luke, "speaking about monkeys, I have a joke that I think this time you will enjoy." And he took advantage of their good nature and continued.

"There was once a bar that was run by monkeys, and they decided to have a contest. A monkey walked in and read the sign that said: "MAKE A HUMAN LAUGH AND WIN $1,000. So the monkey took a man and went around the back, then everyone heard the man laughing. People were amazed because no monkey had ever done that before! Two days later the bar had a sign that said, "MAKE A HUMAN LAUGH AND CRY AND WIN $2,000." So the same monkey that won before took another man around back and everyone heard the man laughing, and shortly afterwards the man started to cry. When they came back in, the bar people were asking: How did he do that? The monkey that was running the contest finally demanded that the other monkey reveal his secret, "No monkey could ever do it and you did it three times!?" Then the monkey said, "Well, I told him I had a bigger penis than he did. The human laughed, so I pulled down my pants!!!"

Both James and Harvey burst into laughter and wouldn't stop for three minutes. And triumphantly Lucas said: "I got ya!"

He was always like that, telling shameless jokes whenever friends got together, and he became known as a sort of comedian. He was a bright and serious person, however, but he just liked to make people laugh.

It became a regular thing afterwards that every week, sometimes on weekends when he stayed over, James got involved more and more with Harvey's social crowd in Colon and Silver City. One Saturday in March 1951 they were in Camp Coiner, and he was introduced to another one of Harvey's brothers. This brother, Carlton Corbin, lived with his wife Beatrice and their three children in Camp Coiner. They took a liking immediately to James because they saw in him a serious, intelligent, warm individual. Carlton even chided his brother Harvey to act a little more serious about life like his friend, and stop some of the carefree, wild behavior he was accustomed to.

Harvey had a girlfriend, Jean, and they already had a child and were not married, although they lived together.

"You have a girlfriend yet, James?" Carlton asked him.

"No," and I am not looking for one right now either," he replied.

"Well, you'd better be careful," said Carlton. "Watch out for traps! They may be looking for you. And with the crowd Harvey hangs out with you never can tell."

"Thanks for the advice," said James.

His wife, Beatrice, a very soft-spoken, pleasant, congenial person brought out some refreshments and you could see the genuine love that existed between the two of them. Their children were in their room doing their homework and were called in to meet the visitor. "These are our three children," said Bea, "This is Sheila 8, Ainsworth 6, and Carlton, Jr. 5," and as they were introduced, they were very polite and smiled at James and each one said respectfully, "How do you do Mr. Edwards. My name is ....," and, "I am pleased to meet you, sir." Then they were sent back to their room to finish their homework.

During the conversation that followed, James asked Carlton what kind of work he does in the Canal Zone.

"I am one of the token black supervisors on the Cristobal docks," he replied. "It's a stressful job most of the time because you must deal with disgruntled workers under you and at the same time with unreasonable white slave drivers over you who are always pushing too hard. If the pay wasn't better than average and I didn't have a wife and children to support, I would have told them off and quit long ago. But I learned to deal with it and stay calm when I want to explode, and smile when I really want to cuss. Why do you think I smoke so many cigarettes? It's to ease the stress. But you didn't come here to hear my complaints. How is Wimpy treating you?"

"Who is Wimpy?" asked James.

"Your principal, that's what I call him because he is a wimp, an Uncle Tom for those white men who run the school system. Wait until one of those white bosses from the central administration comes around and you'll see what I mean. Ask Harvey here about him. He knows him."

"That's not fair," said Harvey, "he does his job well and he takes good care of the school; he can account for every penny spent, and he doesn't ruffle any feathers. Sometimes he can be a little sneaky, though. My friends tell me he always sneaks up on them like he thinks they are going to steal the school building, or they are doing something wrong. He doesn't mess with the veteran teachers, though. In fact, he depends on them, especially his able assistant, to keep things in order and running smoothly. So don't pick on my friend."

"To answer your question," interjected James, "I get along with him and with everyone else. I don't have any problems."

"That's probably because you are an excellent teacher, and you make him look good. Anyway, I guess some people just aren't meant to be leaders. He's one of them."

"You know, Carlton," said Harvey, "Jim was asking me why they have so many different silver towns and camp towns like Silver City, Silver City Heights, and towns like Camp Beard, Camp Coiner, etc. when they are all in the same Cristobal District, we are not in the army, and we are mostly black people of the same Caribbean origin and live in close proximity to each other. Also, why do they call the river Folks River? Could you speak on that?"

"Sure," said Carlton, "but I am going to have to give you a little history lesson. I may not be a schoolteacher, but I read a lot about history, especially when it comes to this town. And don't think I am trying to school you either because I am not; you are too intelligent for that. Anyway, this is what I know from my own research. Colon is a city that was built by the Panama Railroad Co. on what was once an uninhabitable island nestled close to the mainland, and it was called Manzanillo Island, a swampy, mangrove-filled, pest- infested island approximately one square mile in area, surrounded by water and located at the entrance to Limon Bay in the Atlantic Ocean. It was surrounded by Limon Bay in the west, the Atlantic Ocean in the north, Manzanillo Bay in the east and Folks River in the south. There was open salt water on all sides of Manzanillo except the southern side, where Folks River formed a narrow channel that separated Manzanillo from the mainland.

On this swampy island tropical vegetation took root, and, as vegetation died it furnished soil that after many, many years of repetition of this process a foot or so of soil raised itself above the surface of the water and supported a swampy jungle of tortuous, water-loving mangroves, interlaced vines and thorny shrubs, and slimy mud fit for alligators and reptiles, sand flies, and mosquitos. Part of the channel became filled in, connecting it to the mainland, and once construction of the railroad began in 1850, the American railroad company brought in thousands of West Indian laborers from Jamaica to work on the railroad tracks. They built shacks to live in that rose up on piles amid the swampy vegetation, and more land was filled in until a solid foundation was created to support the machine shops and railroad buildings. As part of the railroad established itself, they gave the town the name of Aspinwall in honor of the founder of the Panama Railroad Company, William Henry Aspinwall, an American businessman.

Gold-digging fortune hunters heading for California gold mines disembarked at manzanillo, later called Colon, caught the train heading for the Pacific side to board a ship in Balboa port heading for

California. When they arrived from the U.S. at this first stop on the Atlantic side, they found that the city of Colon, at that time a shanty town mostly on stilts, was crowded with saloons, bars, stores along Front Street, prostitutes, gambling houses, brothels, and bars on Bottle Alley. Most of the streets were barely above tide level, unpaved and strewn with garbage, broken glass and furniture, dead animals, and squalor. Most of the town was reeking with putrefaction and disease.

When the French, who signed an agreement with Columbia, took over in 1879 under Ferdinand de Lesseps to build a French canal, Colon didn't change much; but the French built up the eastern shore and called it Christophe-Colomb (which later became Cristobal) and made it look a little neater with a number of one-story buildings, white with green shutters, enclosed by verandas. These were the cottages for white officials and technicians.

Most of Colon, nevertheless, remained for a very long time still a swampy and mangrove-filled place even after the railroad was built. A "pest hole" is what they called it. The pest hole remained a pest hole until the U.S. took over the construction of the Panama Canal from the French in 1904. They completely drained the rest of the swamp, filled it in and raised it with landfills from the Panama Canal excavations, sanitized it by getting rid of pests and diseases, laying paved streets, building a sewerage system, a clean water system, a cold storage plant, etc. and made it livable. It was no longer an island but was now connected to the mainland with only three sides open to the sea, Limon Bay, the Atlantic Ocean and Manzanillo Bay. They changed its name from Aspinwall to Colon in honor of Cristobal Colon. For all the good that the U.S. did in building up the city and the Canal Zone, of course they also brought racial discrimination and segregation with them, too.

As for your second question, Folks River was originally named Fox River (I think it was shaped like a fox's head). Before the U.S. acquired the rights from Panama in 1904 to build the canal, the French had put up some small portable houses in bad condition between the railroad shops and the main train line. By 1915 the people who lived near Fox River changed its name to Folks River, mispronouncing it over the years as people often do with names. The place you call Silver City was originally a landfill at the Folks River end of Manzanillo Island. They used the soil taken from the excavation of the Panama Canal and when they were building Fort Davis. At that time, 1921, they called it Cristobal's "Silver Town" for silver workers (West Indians) and their families on the Canal Zone, since they had no intention of having blacks live in the same town with whites in Cristobal, Margarita, and Coco Solo, etc. Later, in 1933, Silver Town or, as the locals called it, Silver City, was expanded to include Silver City Heights, and, after the 1940 Colon fire decimated a half of Colon and created a large number of refugees among Panama Canal workers who lived in Colon, the area across Randolph Road that was occupied by the U.S. military in WW II was converted to a civilian Canal Zone town with army buildings replaced by experimental housing for silver workers, and they kept the name Camp Coiner. It is the second civilian suburb of Silver City, but it is still not enough space because more expansion is needed since they don't have enough quarters yet, even with Camp Coiner, to house all the refugees and, especially, to house all those families they are trying to relocate from Camp Beard, which is an overcrowded barracks not fit for families to live in and which I am told the U.S. government is going to demolish soon anyway. They are planning to clear some more land adjacent to Silver City to build more houses, some new types of duplex houses for silver workers and their families within a year or so. They are clearing the land right now to start construction and they are going to so much trouble, believe me, simply because they don't want to integrate black and white people. But I don't have to tell you that, you know what kind of dual system we live in in every Canal Zone town across the Isthmus.”

“Wow,” said James, “I am amazed at how much you know about the subject.”

“You must know something about your history, otherwise people will lie about it and take advantage of you. I make sure my children are going to know as much as I can teach them. You’re a schoolteacher, how comes you never knew all these things already?”

“I admit that I am not too familiar with the history of how Colon province and Cristobal district were formed, but I do know that long before Manzanillo was habitable, Columbus had landed on the Atlantic shores just a few miles east of Manzanillo in 1502 on his fourth voyage. He named the inlet Puerto Bello, which is now called Portobelo (which port was used by Spain as a warehouse where they stored, and from where they shipped gold and other tropical goods and raw materials back to Spain) and Columbus continued mistakenly to think that he had reached the Indies by travelling west, as Marco Polo had done earlier when he traveled east in the opposite direction through Asia; and I know that all of Central America, including the Isthmus of Panama, was once ruled by Spain until Simon Bolivar, by the year 1824, had liberated Columbia and the rest of Central and South America from Spain; and in 1903 the U.S. military, applying its gunboat diplomacy, had forced Columbia out of Panama so that the U.S. could make a deal to their liking with the newly created Panamanian government for the rights to build the Panama Canal. But, of course, I don't need a lecture on U. S. Canal Zone racism since I was born in it, and I know a little about the history of La Boca and other Pacific towns like Red Tank and Paraiso and Gamboa (Santa Cruz). I've also studied a little about our African heritage and how we came to be here in the Isthmus of Panama in the first place, all of which I am sure you must know since you, too, are a student of our history. But today, thanks to you, I have learned a lot about how the province of Colon and the District of Cristobal and its communities, both black and white, came to be what they are today."

"You know," said Carlton, "if any of my children transfer to Silver City Elementary School, I am going to insist that they are assigned to your class. They can learn a great deal from you. Between us both, you their teacher and my wife and I their parents, how can they miss? Incidentally, I don't agree with naming adjacent black communities with "silver" names and "camp" names, either. To me, that fosters segregation among us as black people and perpetrates the slave/master race mentality so they can divide and conquer us much easier. If we want unity among ourselves, we should have one name that better identifies us as one people and brings us closer together -- and I don't mean a name with 'silver' in it which they used to demean us or the name of a camp honoring some white soldier who is the last thing West Indians need to be associated with. Maybe one day we will see the light and change that situation."

And with that the subject of history was no longer on the table. James took Carlton's remarks as a compliment which he would like to get from all the parents of the students he teaches. Of course, he has received numerous compliments already, but Carlton Corbin's was the best so far.

Chapter VII:

Iona Reid and Her Dilemma

In a certain part of Silver City lived the Reid family. Rufus Reid, a Barbadian, was employed in the Mount Hope cold storage plant. He was married to Sephora Reid, also from Barbados, and together they had three children, Iona 24, Ilene 21, and Rufus, Jr.19. Rufus, Sr. was in his fifties, a mild-mannered man, very quiet and passive in nature compared to his younger wife who was in her forties. Sephora was somewhat attractive, outgoing, a bit flirty, cunning, domineering, determined, disarmingly sweet and friendly. Rufus Sr. would come straight home from work every day, sit in his rocking chair, read his newspapers, and on the weekend in the dry season he would go out to play cricket. He relished those occasions away from home when he seemed to actually enjoy himself and become animated on the cricket field.

One morning after Rufus left for work, Sephora and Iona were alone in the living room of their home.

"Your sister is getting married next month," Sephora said to Iona, "your brother is working and will soon be on his own. You are the oldest child and tell me, what are you doing with your life? You've got a little "pickney" to feed and no husband. You can't stay up in here forever expecting us to go on supporting you and your baby. You had better go and find a husband to take care of you. You hear what I say?"

And Sephora went storming out the door dressed to kill, though she claimed she was only going to the market for a few things. But she laid her mind out plain to her eldest child who had been sitting around in the house too long like she had no worries in the world. Well, Sephora wasn't going to stand for that any longer. It's a good thing the little girl was in the bedroom sleeping and didn't hear anything that was said. But Iona got the message. Yes, she would like to get from under her mother's domination, her nagging all the time and her constant chastisement for her mistake. Only she didn't know what to do. She consulted with her girlfriend Marlene for some advice.

"Marlene, I don't know what to do. I am going to go crazy the way my mother never lets me forget what happened."

"Do you have a boyfriend?" asked Marlene.

"No."

"How old is your little girl?"

"Melia is three."

"There are only two ways that could solve your problem. Either you find a job – in which case I would help you with the babysitting since I am home taking care of my three babies – or you must find a husband candidate and get married."

"I tried the first one without success since I lost my job in the Cristobal commissary," said Iona, "but I can keep trying again. The second choice is almost impossible."

"Nothing is impossible, child. But it will be if you don't try. Can you come by tomorrow evening around 6 p. m., I'm sure your mother wouldn't mind your trying to get help and would be glad to take care of your daughter while you are doing so. A couple of my girlfriends are going to come by my apartment tomorrow evening and together we'll talk and see what we can come up with. Don't worry, we'll think of something." And she hung up the phone after Iona agreed to come by.

"Come here, Melia," Iona called to her three-year old daughter out of wedlock. "We are going to clean up and go out for a walk, okay sweetie?"

Sephora returned just as Iona and her daughter were getting ready to leave the house.

"Where are you going? You have money to spend that I don't know about?"

"I am just going for a walk with my daughter. I need to go out for a little while."

"That's a good idea. Go walking by that elementary school. I see they have some young schoolteachers there who might be looking for a wife. You look nice enough. You are still a good catch. Go on and here's some change if you need to stop and buy some candy for Melia on the way. Now go on."

The next day when she got to Marlene's there were three other ladies there to whom Marlene introduced her.

"Iona, meet Norma, Myrna, and Jean whom I believe you already know."

She said hello and they all returned the greeting. Then she spoke to Jean, the youngest in the group.

"We used to be in the same homeroom and took some classes together. Remember Ms. McDonald our Spanish teacher? I used to like her class a lot."

"Yes, that was four years ago when we attended Jr. High classes together. I used to think that you would come back and enroll in the new High school that opened in '49."

"No, I got a job in the Cristobal Commissary near Front Street where I worked for a few years."

Marlene interrupted as she placed some refreshments on the table.

"Now that we have gotten the introductions out of the way, besides our usual girl talk we'd like to see if we can concentrate on helping Iona. She has a problem. Some of us have either already gone through what she is experiencing, or we know someone who has. You want to tell them Iona or you want me to?"

"It's kind of hard for me right now," said Iona, "it's even harder for me to say it. I am living at home with my parents as a single mom and I have a little girl to take care of."

"Aren't you getting any help from the baby father?" asked Jean.

"A little but that good-for-nothing didn't tell me that he had a wife and family before he made me pregnant and then abandoned me to catch hell at home from my parents. I can't tell you what I went through and am still going through."

"How old is your daughter?" asked one of the ladies.

"Melia is three years old."

"In my situation," said Myrna, "I guess I am a little more fortunate. The baby's father not only stepped up, but he is also helping me take care of our little boy, and he said he is going to marry me, but we haven't set a date yet. I hear my father dropping hints sometimes like 'He'd better hurry up and make up his damn mind. That's what happens when these young people today have babies before they get married. Most of the times they don't.'"

"What about you, Norma?" asked Marlene.

"I am like you," said Norma, "I am happily married with two children, a boy and a girl, but I sympathize with a lot of girls that are taken advantage of by men who can't control their libido and keep their privates in their pants. Most of them are just like street dogs looking to hump on any female that passes by. There should be a law against getting a girl pregnant and then leaving her alone to face the consequences."

"Anyway," said Marlene, "a woman must find a way to survive no matter what. She has to be practical and do whatever she has to do to survive, especially when she has offspring to take care of. Don't you all agree with me?"

"Of course," added Norma, "we women must stick together and help each other. My best advice to Iona is to get involved socially, go out some more, go to parties, dances, festivities, and places where you can meet men, I mean decent men, and use what charms God gave you to catch one of them -- just play the game so you don't get hurt. You know the saying, 'All is fair in love and war.' You'd be surprised to see the things some women do to catch a man. And I don't care how many children they already have. If they still look good and sexy and can arouse men's libido, they've got a good chance like any woman. All you must do is be smart and play the game to win."

They all agreed with this line of thinking. As to which alternative was the better one, getting a job first or finding a husband, they didn't want to exclude one or the other.

"Finding a husband who can take care of you," said Marlene, "should be the first choice in these times, but if you can find a job, too, in the meantime, that can help to put food on the table."

"The only problem with the second option, though," said Norma as an afterthought, "is that the situation today is a little bleak with a lot of layoffs taking place and finding a job, especially for a woman, is so hard."

"I agree with Norma," said Iona, "although some people might say I am not trying hard enough."

"You might want to check out that new 'Zona Libre' they are starting in France Field," said Jean. "You never know, they're talking about it; in fact, it's more than talk now, three years ago, in 1948, President Enrique Jimenez had signed the law and they've since started building it and they are going to need a lot of workers."

"What do you know about the Zona Libre? What is that all about?" asked Norma.

"The Free Zone, or more correctly, the Free Trade Zone (or international free port) is a section of Colon near Manzanillo Bay entrance from the Atlantic Ocean where the Panamanian government is constructing storage facilities and is inviting foreign countries to warehouse their merchandise there, sell them wholesale, duty-free, to merchants who re-export the goods from the Free Zone to customers throughout Latin America and the Caribbean and other places without the original shipper having to pay expensive import/export duty taxes and costs to reach their customers. Operating in the Free Trade Zone, companies, in addition to avoiding import/export duty taxes as previously mentioned, pay no taxes to Panama on their profits; they only pay a fixed charge for permits, security, garbage collection, forms (paperwork), and rental space in the zone. Companies can quickly ship their goods north and south through the Canal from there and they can access trade routes by sea and air leading anywhere, including countries in Asia, Australia, and Europe.

Merchants and/or customers come to Panama and buy in one place goods from different countries at a cheaper price in the zone. You know what that means? They will build thousands and thousands of stores and warehouses that are going to need thousands and thousands of managers, clerical, sales, food service and warehouse type workers. They are starting with a small area now of about a few acres but, if you ask me, eventually they are going to take over all of Colon.”

“Yeah, but that’s not happening tomorrow. Who knows when that will happen and when all those jobs will be available?” replied Norma.

“Well at least you can find out and it wouldn’t hurt to fill out a job application form in any case.”

“That’s an option for you to check out, Iona, just in case. But getting back to what we were saying before, and don’t get me wrong when I say this, you desperately need a man.”

“I am sure my mother would agree with you. That’s all she keeps harping about.”

And they started to lighten up a bit and joke about all the possible eligible men around and how to catch one. Just then Lucas, Marlene’s husband, entered the apartment and with his usual comedic charm chided them.

"Good evening my fine and fancy fair ones of the opposite sex," he says to them as he kisses his wife, "you are all in good spirits, I hope. Here's a quote from a famous chanticleer: 'Whenever you see more than two hens get together, roosters had better beware!'" then he says, while looking sideways at Marlene, "Should this good rooster be worried about anything?"

"No, you rascal you with your funny remarks," said Marlene. "We are nice ladies; we are not like you sneaky men" (dropping him a hint that he alone knows what she means). "Anyway, what we are about is none of your business. You better leave us alone!"

"That's right, Marlene," says Norma. "Tell that troublemaker to go away!"

And as he walked away, they all started laughing because they knew the way he was, always coming up with some funny remark. The ladies were finishing up their meeting just before he stepped in anyway, and they got up to leave.

"I think we made a good start tonight," said Marlene. "Let's keep in touch and meet again soon. We've got to help our sister here solve her problem."

They all agreed and said goodnight as they called out to Lucas who had slipped into the kitchen.

"Goodnight troublemaker!!"

And he answered back.

"Good night nice ladies!! Get home safely!"

Chapter VIII:

The Birthday Party for Francis Bingham

Two days after the meeting at Marlene's she got a call from Theresa Bingham, a close friend of all four ladies, asking her to convey to the others a special invitation by word of mouth. Immediately afterwards, Marlene called Norma.

"Norma, Theresa Bingham just called me to tell me she is planning a 41st birthday party for her husband, Francis, at her home on April 14, 1951, a week from this Saturday and doesn't have time to send out formal invitations. She was only inviting her closest friends, meaning us. She asked me to contact you and said she would like us to also bring our spouses or boyfriends and to call her back and confirm."

"That's such a coincidence with what we were discussing the other evening," said Norma to Marlene over the phone. We have to make sure that Iona comes."

"Yes, and what we must do is to get her a date or else invite a few single men for her to meet. I am going to call her right now."

Iona was glad to be invited and promised to be there.

"It will give me time to get my hair done and I know my mother will be glad to hear about it," said Iona.

"It's about time," said Sephora when she told her about the plan. "That's what you have to do instead of sitting up in the house all the time. You think men are going to come here looking for you; you must go out where they can see you. And wear something sexy."

When Marlene spoke to Jean, Jean told her that Theresa had already called her and she told Theresa both she and her fiancée, Bob, were going to come.

"Lucas Corbin," Marlene said to her husband Luke, "we are going to a birthday party a week from this Saturday night so don't make any commitments for that evening."

"Who is giving the party?"

"Our mutual friend, Theresa Bingham is having a birthday party for her husband. You know her and Francis very well. That's your buddy, remember?"

"O yes, yes, of course, Francis is my man. We play cricket together sometimes."

And to make sure she covered all the bases she gave Harvey Corbin a call as well.

"Hello, Harvey, this is Marlene."

"Hi, Marlene, what's up?"

"On behalf of Theresa Bingham I am inviting you and Jean to her house party on Saturday, April 14, 1951, to celebrate her husband's 41st birthday. I hope you haven't made any other commitments for that date."

"That's a week from this Saturday, right?"

"Yes. And bring that schoolteacher friend of yours, too. Can I count on you Harvey?"

"Yes. No problem. I'm sure there'll be some single girls there for him as well."

"There'll be single ones and coupled ones. Don't worry."

And with that Marlene felt sure that she had done her duty to help her friend out.

At the party many people were there, including some of Francis' friends and some of Theresa's friends; and the guest of honor was accorded birthday greetings by all the guests as they entered. There were well over 2 dozen people, mostly couples and 4 singles including Iona and another single lady friend of Theresa's, Maria, and two single men that Marlene had invited, James and a friend of Lucas named Cyrus. Theresa asked Marlene to help her and both of them went around the room introducing people who were strangers to get everyone acquainted, and, of course, Marlene was especially sure to introduce James and Iona to each other. She even whispered in James's ears, "She is by herself, so you don't have to worry about jealous boyfriends or husbands." That way she planted a seed and hoped that it would take root.

Ever the gentleman, James was cordial to Iona and initiated a conversation.

"I guess we are the only ones in the room who are not hitched to anyone, at least not to anyone in this room."

"Nor outside either," replied Iona. "At least I can speak for myself, what about you?"

Instead of playing the game of cat and mouse she didn't waste any time letting him know right away where she stood. He was a little bit taken off guard by her quick response though.

"Is... is that... an invitation?"

"You can take it to mean whatever you want," said Iona.

"Well, I just want to have a good time and you seem to want the same thing, too, obviously."

Just at that moment James was asked by Harvey to excuse himself and he told Iona he would be right back, although, in his mind, James was grateful to Harvey for the interruption. At the same time, Marlene grabbed Iona's arm and pulled her into the kitchen where Norma and Jean were waiting.

"Tell us what you think about him?" asked Marlene and Norma.

"Well, I think he is fine, but I might have moved too fast. He hesitated when I tried indirectly to find out if he was committed to anyone."

"What do you expect, you just met him," said Marlene.

"Yeah, you know how men are," said Norma, "they don't want you to know their business, but you must tell them yours."

Meanwhile, a few of the men with drinks in their hands had huddled in one corner of the room telling each other funny jokes. One man, Phillip, whose wife was helping Theresa in the kitchen, told the following.

"Two men went fishing when one decided to have a smoke. He asks the other one if he has a light. He replies, "Yes, I do!" and hands him a 10-inch-long RONSON lighter. Surprised, the first man asks, "Geeze, where did you get this?" The second man replies, "Oh I have a personal genie who grants wishes." "Can I make a wish with your genie?" "Sure," says the second man, "just make sure that you speak clearly because he is a little hard of hearing." "Ok, I will," says the first man. As he rubs the magic lamp a genie appears and asks the man what he wants. He says to the genie, "I want a million bucks." The genie says, "OK," and goes back into the lamp and 10 seconds later a million ducks fly overhead. And the first man says to the second man, "Your genie really sucks with his hearing, doesn't he?" The second man replies, "I know, do you really think I asked for a 10-inch RONSON?"

And so as not to be outdone, Lucas had to jump in and tell one of his jokes, too, which he always loves to do.

"An elderly Bajan lady," says Luke, "is in an elevator in a high- rise apartment building in New York City going to visit some relatives. A beautiful young woman gets in smelling like very expensive perfume. She turns up her nose at the elderly woman and says arrogantly, "Guerlain Shalimar $120.00 an ounce."

The elderly lady with a deadpan expression says nothing.

Another young and beautiful woman smelling expensive enters the elevator, turns, looks down her nose at the old lady and says, "Chanel No. 5, Paris, $200.00 an ounce."

The elevator is now filled with the aroma of the magnificent scents of the combined perfumes.

One floor later as the elderly Bajan lady approaches her destination, she quietly eases herself with a long, audible burst of gas, pshhhhhhhhh, which quickly overpowers the combined expensive perfumes and leaves the two young women with water in their eyes.

As the Bajan lady steps out of the elevator, she turns to them and says, "Breadfruit, Barbados, 26 cents a pound."

And that, like the previous jokes, brought hearty laughter.

Just then Theresa and Marlene came over to them who looked like they were having a good time all by themselves.

"What's going on over here?" says Theresa, "this is a party. You had better start engaging these women, wives especially, or you're going to have a big problem when you get home tonight. The women are getting angry and jealous!"

All the guilty husbands and boyfriends knew exactly what that meant and very quickly jumped to make amends as the music player started to sound off some sweet mambo music and Theresa called to everyone to "Get up and dance. Let's have a party!"

And everyone joined in whether they could dance or not and the husbands and boyfriends made sure to sweeten their partners and make them very happy the rest of the evening. And the only singles in the room paired off with each other, James with Iona and Cyrus with Maria as well as all the couples until everybody was letting their hair down and the place was swinging, and everyone was feeling good.

Then the birthday cake was brought out and cut, cards and gifts were opened and read, toasts and speeches were made and, of course, before all the speeches and well wishes were finished, Lukas also had to make a toast. Only this time he was not comedic but more serious than he usually is.

"Let's everybody raise his/her glass one more time please," he said, "I'm going to make a toast to my friend Francis, one of the nicest people I know. Here's to my friend Francis:"

"May your voyage through life be as happy and free, as the dancing waves of the deep blue sea.

May you ride the crest of the waves of life above the troughs of trials and strife, and may you look as young in the years to come as you look tonight at forty-one.

HAPPY BIRTHDAY!!!"

And everyone echoed in unison with glasses raised the age-old phrase and sang the tune "H-A-P-P-Y B-I-R-T-H-D-A-Y T-O Y-O-U."

The dancing resumed and the party continued until 2 a.m. when the guests began to leave, and Marlene turned to James before he could slip away and asked him if he could escort Iona home. Being a gentleman as he was, he said he would and so they left the party together.

They took a taxi and when they arrived at Reid's residence of course Sephora was still up. She wouldn't miss meeting this young single schoolteacher for anything. James asked the taxi to wait and dropped Iona off at her door. Sephora made sure the front door light was on so she could see his face.

"Hello Mrs. Reid. I brought your daughter home safely as you can see. Good night, Iona and Good night, Mrs. Reid."

"Yes," she said. "I wish it was earlier so I could invite you in, but maybe next time. Iona, make sure you bring him by the house for a visit."

"Ma," said Iona, feeling a little embarrassed, and she stopped short of telling her mother anything more that she didn't want to hear. "Goodnight, James," said Sephora as he turned to leave. He got into the cab that took him to Bolivar highway and straight to his Mount Hope address.

In his thoughts just before slipping off to sleep that night he felt it was a nice party; he liked all the people he met, and he enjoyed himself very much. Then he had the thought, "She is nice and all that (meaning Iona), but she's not the girl for me that I want to take home to meet my mother." And with that thought he fell right off to sleep.

The next morning, Sunday, April 15, 1951, he got up too late to make the 11a.m. mass in Colon, and he spent the rest of the morning tidying up and going over his lesson plans for the following week. On Monday when he ran into Harvey of course Harvey wanted to know how he had liked the party.

"It was a great party," he told him. "So far Colon has not disappointed me. I had a great time."

And Harvey told him, "You'd better plan on staying over more often because we have a lot planned for you in the future. When Colon is through with you, you'll be so much at home you will feel like

a native-born son, and you might never want to go
back to Panama City again."

Chapter IX:

James Meets Lisa

Harvey was right about Colon, people there are very open and friendly, very stylish, hospitable and uninhibited and they love to party and enjoy themselves. If during his first three years he was a little slow in getting around, in the next school year, 1951-1952, that all changed, better later than never. He was determined to take more time to get around the city on his own, even venturing to stay over more often on weekends to participate in recreational and social events. With this new attitude he saw the first four months, August to November 1951 go by very quickly with him having been to several baseball games, boxing matches, parades, concerts, and even a bridge game or two at the homes of some new friends. At that rate it didn't take long before that kind of exposure led to something serious. It happened on a Monday evening, December 10, 1951, when he was looking for a tailor shop to have a pair of trousers altered. He came upon a laundry and dry-cleaning establishment that was not his intended stop but for some unknown reason he decided to go in there anyway. As he did, who is to say that what took place was mere chance or wasn't destiny waiting to happen. He entered, and there she was standing before him, an angel smiling at him from behind the counter, and for the first time in his life he did not know what words to say to someone so beautiful. Her face was like an image from Heaven. He was instantly frozen in time when she smiled, and he was lost for words as her crystal-clear eyes of amber looked straight into his and she spoke.

"Don't just stand there now; we don't have all day to wait on you. What is your business, Sir? Come on, come on!"

She wasn't being harsh or mean or anything like that. In fact, it was more like a friendly, pleading way she spoke to him because he just stood there for a few minutes like a statue gazing at her, like he had lost his mind or his voice and had gone to Heaven and was absent from the body for a little while before he could say three words.

"I am sorry!"

"I don't know what you are sorry for," she said, "but please, I can't wait on you all day. We receive, clean and deliver laundry, pants, shirts, dresses, suits, etc. Do you have any of those to drop off? Or any receipts for clothes to pick up? And what is that you have in your bag there? Let me see it now."

And he did as she requested and placed on the counter the bag containing the trousers he was taking to be altered.

"That's all the clothes you've got?" she asked.

"Yes," he said, "but I have plenty more at home. If you like, I can..."

And she stopped him before he could finish the sentence.

"That won't be necessary. We only clean dirty clothes; when they get dirty you can bring them in. Even this pair of trousers doesn't look dirty to me, what did you want to dry clean them for?"

"Do you do alterations, too?"

"Yes, is that what you want done?"

"Yes. Please shorten the length 2 inches and put a cuff on it please and press it afterwards."

She sensed by then that he wasn't a silly or confused young man, but that it was she, somehow, who was having a strange effect on him to cause him to act silly and confused, and she was amused by it, too, for a while. Then she got serious and asked him for his name and address for the Dry-Cleaning customer records that they kept on all their customers. He gave her his address in Mt. Hope where he stayed. She knew for certain that he was no fool;

in fact, he was one of those young schoolteachers that she remembered seeing many times during her junior and senior years at Silver City Occupational High School. Sometimes she used to see him walking neatly dressed in a white shirt and tie by the high school building. Several times, he even came onto the high school campus, but he never noticed her. She had noticed him, though, and he looked cute, but he seemed to be very shy. Once he came into her high school classroom to visit his pal, that Mr. Harvey Corbin, who was her English teacher, and she remembers how she and a classmate of hers had gossiped in class about him when they saw him and wondered what it would take to get his attention -- he seemed so serious and scholarly. Now, as he stood there right before her very eyes, she was so enjoying the exchange that she pretended as hard as she could not to know who he was and not to take him seriously.

"Look," she said, "here's the receipt for the alteration and pressing. It will be ready in three business days. The amount is written on the receipt, and you can pay for it when you pick up the trousers on Wednesday the 12th. So, I'll see you on Wednesday. Okay?"

"Yes," he replied with a smile, and he thanked her for being kind, tucked the receipt into his pocket and headed for Silver City to keep a dinner appointment.

On the afternoon of Wednesday, December 12th after teaching his last class and after finishing preparations for the next day's lessons, he hung around the school with some of his colleagues and left the building after 5 p.m. On his way home he stopped by the cleaners to pick up his trousers. He could not wait to get there; after all, she had been on his mind constantly since the last time he saw her.

When he arrived at the store she was there, and she seemed happy to see him. She was beaming and smiling.

"I see you didn't forget to return to pick up your trousers today although you are a little bit late, we are closing in fifteen minutes."

"I am sorry; I didn't realize that you close at 6 p.m. I'll try to come earlier next time."

He handed her the receipt and waited for his package. When he received the package and paid for it, he said to her:

"Since it's almost 6 o'clock, do you mind if I wait for you and walk with you to the bus stop? That is, if your boyfriend isn't going to meet you?"

Were he just another forward woman chaser she would have told him something unpleasant, but she had taken such a liking to him before from the first time she had seen him on campus that, without hesitation, she answered him in the affirmative.

"I don't have a boyfriend and it's alright if you care to wait."

At 6:10 p.m. they were walking together to the bus stop conversing for he seemed to have found his voice and mind again although her beauty still affected him, and he was going in the wrong direction.

"Aren't you taking the bus to Mount Hope? Mount Hope is in that direction opposite to where I am going. I am going towards Randolph Rd. in Silver City Heights. Your bus stop is on the next block in that direction west of here."

But he didn't care which direction was which, he only knew he didn't want to part with her company so soon.

"Don't they turn around and come back so I can change buses? I could ride with you and come back after you get off at your stop. It's just that I never met anyone like you since I arrived in Colon, and I would like to at least get to know your name."

And as he spoke her eyes met his and her thoughts began to examine all the possibilities for, she, too, had not met anyone quite like him either. He was so handsome, clean cut, and innocent, an educated young man, and a schoolteacher with a bright future besides.

When the bus arrived, they boarded and sat together in the back of the bus as they continued their conversation.

"Well, James Edwards, that is, if you gave your correct name on the form, my name is Lisa Peterson and I live in Silver City Heights. And you know where I work 5 days a week including Saturdays."

"How long have you been working there?"

"Six months since I graduated from high school."

"You mean Silver…"

And she finished the sentence for him:

"Yes, Silver City Occupational High School, the class of June 1951, and I guess you are one of those new teachers from out of town that everybody has been talking about?"

"That depends on what you mean by new. I have been teaching at Silver City Elementary School for almost three years now since graduating from La Boca

Normal Training School. I must have been blind not to have seen you before during that time."

"Not blind, just too serious and busy to notice me, even though the high school and the elementary school are very close to each other. Nevertheless, while you were so blind, I remember seeing you several times when you came over to the high school to visit."

To show how women are, she already had her eyes on him when he strutted around the high school campus on several occasions in the past, and he didn't even know it.

"Well, I am not blind now," he was quick to add. "I am seeing you with all the vision that God gave me, and I've never seen clearer or better in my life."

She was flattered and his words made her feel warm inside and a little frightened, too, that she might give away too soon how she felt toward him.

"This stop coming up is mine so don't bother to get up. Remember you were staying on the bus until you got back to your stop." And before he could react, she got off the bus which quickly pulled away. They waved to each other as it did.

For the next two days, especially on the job, she couldn't get him out of her mind, and she saw his face everywhere she turned until her supervisor had to tell her to stop daydreaming and pay attention to her work.

She was hoping she would get to see him again soon, and for that matter she did not have to wait long. Saturday morning at 11 a.m. he came into the laundry and dry-cleaning store, and he had with him a good size bag of clothes he brought to be laundered and pressed. She was so happy to see him, and very curious.

"You dirtied all those clothes already in just 2 days since last Wednesday? How in Heaven did you do that?"

"Well, I don't know," he said, "but how else was I going to see you again?"

Of course, he didn't tell her that he had begged some of his friends to give him their dirty shirts and pants to have cleaned at his expense and they weren't to ask any questions, that he was returning favors he owed them. That's how he got those dirty clothes.

"Whatever you did you must have gone to an awful lot of trouble just so you could see me again," she said.

"The male of all species do strange and foolish things sometimes," James replied. "For instance, do you know why the King bird in nature does many flip flops and summersaults? And the red-capped manikin bird, for another example, does strange moon walks?"

"No, why?" asked Lisa.

"I don't think they even know themselves, but they act that way whenever they see a female they like very much and want her for a mate."

"Well," she replied, caught a little off guard by his remark, "all I can say...is...I... bet... that... by now you have run out of dirty shirts and pants." She said this almost stammering and in a joking manner.

"Lisa, even if I have no more shirts and pants, can I still come by and do for you some summersaults and moonwalks like the King bird and the Manikin? Or I could recite some poetry to you, whichever you prefer."

"That's very funny," said Lisa laughing, and she was even prettier when she laughed.

"You don't have to do all that," she added, "all you have to do is ask me nicely if you want to see me, and if I feel like it, I will say yes. Otherwise, it doesn't matter what you do."

"I hope I didn't ruin my chances then by acting like a fool. Lisa, will you let me see you again then, and perhaps let me take you for a walk, or to dinner, or to a movie or a ballgame if you like sports or anything else you would prefer?"

"If it's a date you are asking me for, I am getting off work early today at 2 o'clock and there's a movie showing at the Caribe theatre that I would like to see. Meet me at 2 p.m. and we'll go and see it, if you like."

Her words pleased his heart and he said he'll see her later.

All the king's horses and all the king's men couldn't keep him from that date. He came promptly at 2 p.m. and was as happy as he could be as they got onto the bus headed for Colon.

When they reached the theatre the movie that was showing was not a "Streetcar Named Desire" as she had hoped. Somehow, they changed the billboard posting and starting that night they were showing a different movie, "Orphee" (Orpheus) in French with subtitles in Spanish. James spoke some French and it was one of Lisa's favorite subjects in school.

"Isn't Orpheus about that love story in Greek mythology where one of the lovers, Eurydice, died and the other, Orpheus, went down into the underworld to find her?" asked Lisa.

"Yes, it is a famous love story," said James.

"I want to see it. I insist, let's go and see it," said Lisa.

James didn't mind, he would have gladly taken her to Heaven if she wanted to go there as long as they were together, so it made no difference to him if she wanted to see Orphee or some other movie. Besides, the story of Orpheus and Eurydice had always fascinated him, and she was in the mood for a good love story.

While they sat in the theatre, he tried at first to keep his hands to himself, but she cozied up to him, put her hands into his and leaned so close against him he felt unspeakable joy. He knew then that she was his soul mate.

After the movie they stopped at a restaurant and had some pastry and exchanged notes about the movie.

"In the movie that's not how the original story was supposed to go," said Lisa.

"No, I agree," said James. They changed it up a lot. In the original story Orpheus was a musician and, in the movie, they made him a writer, a poet."

"And" said Lisa, "they made the master of the underworld, Death, a woman who possessed people's bodies (or souls) after they died and made them do her bidding. Her henchmen were the ones who ran

Eurydice down in the street in the first place and killed her and when Orpheus succeeded in crossing into the land of the dead to bring her back, he had to appear before some judges there who told him that he could take Eurydice back with him, but he must never look at her face again. How could anyone live together with their loved one without ever looking at her face? Tell me, if you were Orpheus and I was Eurydice could you spend the rest of your life with me without looking at my face?"

"Of course not," said James, "that would be impossible to do."

"They knew that, too," said Lisa, "but they were following the orders of their boss, that woman, Death. Naturally, Orpheus eventually broke down and looked at Eurydice's face and lost her. Then I couldn't understand what happened next. It seemed to me that Death was in love with Orpheus all along and she was behind Orpheus and Eurydice's deaths, but in the end, she had a change of heart and sent them back to the living to live out their lives. I don't think the producer of this movie did a good job of sticking to the original story. He made it look like a dream or something. It was a little confusing to me."

"You are right" said James, "in the original story Orpheus and Eurydice were happily married to each other. Eurydice was walking in the woods one day and a jealous suitor was chasing after her when a poisonous snake bit her and she died. Orpheus, the son of Apollo the God of music and song, to whom Apollo bequeathed his gift of music and song, could not live without Eurydice and was in such despair that the only music he could make was sad music. His father told him to go down into the underworld to find her. With his lyre he charmed his way there and when he approached Hades, the lord of the underworld, and his wife, Persephone, the music he played was so enchanting that Hades, too, was moved and told him he could take Eurydice back to earth with him but on one condition: She was to follow behind him and he was not to look back at her until he had reached to the upper world. If he looked back too soon, he would lose Eurydice forever. They were almost successful as they were just about to re-enter the upper world when, although he knew that she must be behind him, he longed so much to give one glance to make sure; then, as they were almost out of danger he turned and saw her face in the dim light, and he held out his hand to grab her but in an instant, she was gone. She had slipped back into the underworld. The only sound he heard then was her faint voice calling to him, "Farewell, Orpheus my love…" and she was lost forever."

"That's a sad story. What happened to Orpheus in the end in the original story?" asked Lisa.

"According to the legend, Orpheus was too broken-hearted to go on living without Eurydice. He wandered aimlessly in the woods calling out to his love, "Eurydice… Eurydice…!" wishing to be with her; and he was attacked and killed by wild beasts that tore his body from limb to limb. It is said that the muses came along and gathered up his limbs and buried them in a sanctuary, a tomb at the foot of Mount Olympus, where his remains still rest to this very day, and the legend also has it that in that place where he is buried the nightingales sing more sweetly than anywhere else on earth."

"Oh, that is so sad and so beautiful," said Lisa who wanted to cry.

"Lisa, I believe that with such a strong love as theirs their souls were united forever, even after death. Don't you believe that, too?"

"Yes, I do, I do," agreed Lisa. "In the movie I also thought that somehow the movie makers were trying in their awkward way to convey that sense of the lovers being united forever."

"In spite of everything, did you like the movie?" asked James.

"Well, it wasn't the one I came to see but I liked it very much. I got to use my little knowledge of French and I learned a little more details about a great love story. Best of all, we got to spend some time together. Next time we'll see the other movie. And thank you very much for an enjoyable repast."

That night after he took Lisa home and he lay in bed she was the last thought in his brain before he fell asleep.

"Yes, Lisa is the right one for me; I will take her home one day to meet my mother," he said to himself as he fell fast asleep.

Chapter X:

James and Lisa Fall in Love

The last week of school, 12/17/51 – 12/21/51, was hectic. Faculty members from out of town were making plans to go home for the holidays. The entire school, teachers and their students, were busy conducting Christmas programs, plays, and festive activities during that week, and most of the teachers were planning to make an early exit on Friday evening to start their 10-day Christmas vacation and return to work on January 2nd in the New Year.

Since James' relatives were expecting him to come home on Friday evening to help with preparations for a special celebration they were planning for his mother's birthday, Saturday, December 22nd and also for Christmas, he and Lisa only had a little time on Thursday for themselves. They decided to take advantage of it and slipped into Colon to window shop while there were many fine displays in the stores all over town. They even passed a florist shop when he went in and bought a rose for her and asked her to wear it in her hair for him, which she did, and she looked so pretty that he kissed her. After window shopping, they stopped in a café for light refreshments, and, as they were enjoying themselves, they thanked each other for their gifts. James gave Lisa a heart-shaped locket and she gave him a silk handkerchief and tie. Along with their Christmas wishes, they shared a dozen kisses before they got up and James took Lisa home.

When he returned to Colon in January 1952, they saw each other more frequently. On weekends, either Saturday or Sunday, they would go for walks on one of the main boulevards as far north as Paseo Washington and cross over to the north shore. If they didn't feel like walking, they would take a cab and drive to the north shore seaside to watch the spectacular view of ships lined up in Colon Harbor and Manzanillo Bay.

"I love to come out here with you," Lisa would say to him, "I love the view and the ocean breeze. Don't you?"

"Yes," James said in reply, "it is a beautiful scene. It is a great wonder, too, to think that the whole world passes right here, literally, through our little Colon and our miraculous Panama Canal!"

One weekend, April 19, 1952, after they left a matinee movie in the early afternoon, they went strolling on Paseo Centenario and were sitting on a park bench in Centennial Park when they heard the most delightful music playing on a Victrola, or it may be a radio. It was the voice of an opera singer singing beautifully as it caught both of their attention at the same time.

"Where is that music coming from?" asked James, "It's such a beautiful voice."

"Yes, and that melody is so lovely!" said Lisa. "What is it called?"

"It's a wedding song, do you like it?"

"I love it. I like the words even better," said Lisa, "Listen...O Promise me that someday you and I will take our love together to some sky..."

"It's a wedding song," repeated James, "it's so beautiful, I wish I could sing it for you."

"Yes, you can, or we could sing a duet if we only knew all the words."

And right then and there in the park he kissed her passionately and she returned his passion in full measure.

"Lisa," he said, "Somewhere I read that there is a pearl of so great a value that you could have all the riches in the world and still would not be able to purchase it, yet, people like you and me can obtain it. It is called Paradise. Lisa, you are that pearl to me."

"Then there must be two such pearls," said Lisa.

And their emotions overwhelmed them so much that only the embarrassment caused by curious passersby, who stopped to watch them, kept them from completely losing themselves. They got up, both of their arms entwined around each other, and walked away knowing that they had sealed a bond between them, and it was just as strong as if it were a wedding vow.

The bond grew stronger and it was helped a great deal by another talent that James possessed. Besides a sense of humor, he often recited little poems to her (poems he had read somewhere or he himself had written) that would make her blush: "I love you, Lisa, like the sunflower loves the sun" or, "I love you, Lisa, for as long as roses bloom and clover has perfume…" or, "I love you, Lisa, until the stars grow old, the sun grows cold, and the leaves of the Judgment Book unfold." One evening as they sat in the park, he took out from his pocket another short poem he had written and handed it to her. He recited the words to her while she read them:

'May God bless you, (Lisa), my love,

watch over you from Heaven above.

Wherever you go, whatever you do,

know that I shall always love you.'"

"I like that very much," said Lisa.

"Let's say those words each night as a prayer to heaven for each other, interchanging our names," said James. "If we say it at the same time, exactly at 11:30 p.m., no matter where we are, whether we are in bed or in some quiet place alone, for just a minute while thinking of each other, it will be lifted up to Heaven simultaneously as one prayer, one wish."

"James, do you really mean that?" asked Lisa.

"Yes," said James, as he kissed her more than once, soulfully, while they embraced on the park bench.

They swore to keep that pledge for the rest of their lives no matter what happens in the future.

Chapter XI:

Sephora's Desperation

The group of ladies who had invited James, through Jean's boyfriend, Harvey, to Francis Bingham's birthday party, kept sending him invitations to other weekend parties and socials but he never responded. Harvey came by James' classroom one evening to find out what was going on, and James told him some story about fulfilling commitments in Panama City on the weekends which limited his stayovers for a while. Of course, this was not entirely true, and Harvey suspected as much, but he decided not to press his suspicions and to accept James' explanation for the time being.

Poor Sephora, meanwhile, was desperate to find a mate for her hopeless bachelorette daughter and this precious eligible bachelor candidate, James, seemed to be slipping away from her grasp. The ladies kept sending him invitations and, sure enough, Sephora saw to that through her circle of friends, with Marlene's help. For this young catch of a bachelor to go single when there were so many hungry, unwed women who were dying to grab him, was a downright shame. He couldn't continue avoiding them and turning them down forever, especially one invitation, in particular, to Harvey's engagement party set for Friday, May 9, 1952, to his long-time girlfriend, Jean. And this time, since the event was set for a Friday evening, because Jean and Harvey were leaving on a trip early the next morning, there was no way he could use the weekend trips home to Panama as an excuse to avoid attending.

On May 2nd, the week before the event, Harvey approached him personally, just before he left for Panama City, and told him about the party and that he was expecting him to attend. James planned to take Lisa with him to the party where he intended to announce, that same night, that they were dating and were engaged, thus, closing the door on all prospective female suitors. Unfortunately, when he talked to Lisa on Monday, May 5th, and he was about to tell her his plans, he hardly got the word party out of his mouth when Lisa interrupted him and told him something he did not expect to hear.

"James, I cannot see you this weekend, unfortunately, because I am taking my mother out of town Friday evening to visit a relative. We will be back Sunday night. Anyway, you were planning to go home this weekend for Mother's Day, May 11, so you don't mind, do you?"

"No, of course not, I don't mind," he said slightly disappointed.

"You look like you were going to say something to me before I interrupted you, what is it, James?"

"It isn't very important. It's just that my friend Harvey Corbin and his girlfriend Jean are having an informal engagement party this coming Friday, and only last Friday, when I was leaving for Panama, Harvey told me about it. He apologized for the late notice saying that he and Jean had decided to have the party at the last minute. That's what I was going to tell you and ask if you wouldn't mind going with me. Since it is on Friday, I thought we could go and leave early so I would still be able to catch the Saturday morning train to Panama. But, now, I'll just have to cancel it."

"No," replied Lisa, "Don't do that, he is your best friend; you should go. I'll get to meet his bride-to-be another time."

"Lisa, I am sorry that you are unable to go to the party. Please give your relative my regards, and I'll see you the weekend after I return from Panama."

So much for his plans! But Lisa was right, Harvey was his best friend for a long time, and he should at least support his best friend on his special occasion. I'm sure his best friend would have done the same for him if their situations were reversed. So, he decided he would go, even if alone, and leave the party early.

Meanwhile, Sephora had been calling Jean (Who knows how many times?), pleading with her to ask James if he wouldn't mind coming by her house to pick up Iona and escort her to the party. Jean obliged her and finally called James at his school the day of the party and asked him to do her a big favor, at the last minute, and escort her girlfriend, Iona. He agreed to do it only because he was going alone, anyway, and he couldn't think of an excuse to say 'no' to Jean. How could he say 'no' to her and then show up at the party alone without offending her. So, on Friday, he went by to pick up Iona -- and who could be happier to see him as he arrived at the door?

"Hello James, it's so good to see you again," said Mistress Reid, "Come in, come in, Iona will be ready in just a few minutes. Come in and meet some of the family."

('...the family?') James felt a little uncomfortable as Sephora introduced him to her husband, Rufus Reid, Sr. and little Melia, Iona's daughter. Mr. Reid then offered him a drink and they chatted briefly while he waited.

"So you are the one," said Mr. Reid, "the schoolteacher right?"

"My name is James Edwards and, yes, I am a teacher."

"You know, I had an uncle back home who was a schoolteacher but he taught Bible classes. You know anything about the Bible?"

"I am afraid I know very little."

"You must read Thessalonians Ch. 4:3 and Proverbs Ch. 18:22"

At that moment Sephora interrupted the conversation.

"She's ready, here she is. She'll make you a good w.... I mean partner, James."

Iona entered the living room dressed to kill. You'd think it was her engagement party they were going to. They left for Camp Coiner where Harvey and Jean were holding the party and, as they were leaving, you could hear Sephora.

"Take care of my daughter and stay out as late as you like and have a good time."

James, somehow, started to have a strange feeling after that. Maybe it was Mr. Reid's first statement, "So you are the one..." or his quoting the Bible, "You must read Thessalonians CH. 4:3 and Proverbs CH. 18:22", or the way Sephora referred to her daughter saying, "She would make you a good w... I mean partner," as if her tongue had slipped, or maybe it was a little bit of guilt creeping into James' conscience. (He hated to think that he was playing into a game in Sephora's head that he didn't consent to play.) He satisfied himself, however, with the thought that he was only consenting to the request of the hostess, Jean, on her special occasion and nothing more.

They got to the party and all of Harvey's, Jean's and Marlene's friends were there, especially the group of female co-conspirators who vowed to help Sephora find a mate for Iona--and James was their main target (even if he didn't know it). The host and hostess were in great spirits. Their announced engagement and future marriage were long overdue, so it was no surprise to everyone that they finally made the leap. During the party, all night long, Iona, with the help and prodding of her allies, was busy holding on to James, hugging him and sticking so close to him that it gave the impression they were going together as a couple. James, who was very reluctant at first, started feeling good and was enjoying the physical attention and flirting of the ladies, that was strongly enhanced by the abundance of liquor they were pouring into him deliberately. They also added a special concoction they had prepared just for him, which apparently was taking its effect, as he started to have that glazy, woozy look—you know, ready for the plucking! He forgot everything about leaving early, and, during the entire evening, there was a general light-headedness and looseness in the room, as the party went on until about 2:00 a.m. when everyone started to leave, most of them, including James, inebriated. Harvey called a cab for James and Iona who seemed tipsy and light-headed. Since Harvey knew the cab driver, he paid him in advance and gave him Iona's address.

When they arrived at Iona's address, everyone there had gone to bed. It must have been a new moon that night because at 2:30 a.m. there didn't seem to be a single star shining, the moon was nowhere in sight, and it was pitch dark. Iona (who seemed to be more in control) dismissed the cab. James was high and offered no resistance. Iona couldn't invite James inside (Which she wanted to do!), so she took him quietly around to the back of the house instead, where the hot smooching got out of hand with Iona taking the lead, since she was as horny as she could be, and more sober than James. She sensed, too, that James' libido was out of his control and that he was lost and vulnerable under her spell, her sensual perfume, her sexuality, and the effects of the specially spiked drinks that they had given him earlier at the party. She grabbed him in her state of physical heat, thus arousing him even more, "Don't be anxious to run off and leave me now...!" She said. And at 2:30

a.m., in the back of her house, in the pitch of darkness, the inevitable took place.

That Saturday morning by some miracle James, still woozy, managed to get back to his bachelor quarters around 4:30 a.m. and everything that had happened between 2:30 a.m. and 4:30 a.m. was a complete blank in his head. He wasn't at all sure about what took place, only that he was feeling a little strange and confused. He was still somewhat groggy, with a disquieting feeling consuming him (now that his head was clearing a little) for having gone to the party in the first place, having been tricked into escorting Iona Reid in the second place, and, in the third place, for allowing himself to be so badly compromised. The heavy drinking, the perfume, the touching... and afterwards... the flirting... the wildness... the heavy breathing in the dark... the smooching... was that sex? My God, what had he done? With those thoughts he flopped into his bed and slept it off and awoke at about 10:00 a.m., frantic, because he had to catch the noon train for Panama City. He showered, hurriedly dressed, took his bags that were already packed from the day before and caught a cab to the train station for the afternoon train to Panama City.

Chapter XII:

The Calm before the Storm

When James arrived in Panama City, about 2:30 p.m., first he stopped by a local flower shop to purchase two dozen roses before heading home to Parque LeFevre, where his mother was happily waiting to see him. As he walked up the stairs his father was the first to greet him.

"Marie," he called to his wife, "your son is here!" then turning to James, "Welcome home, son, it's good to see you."

"It's good to see you, too, Dad."

And his mother came towards him as he held the bouquet in one hand and she gave him a big hug.

"These flowers are for you, mom, they should fit nicely in that lovely vase on your dining room table."

"I knew my son would not forget me, even though you are a little late. I thought you said you were coming on the early train, what happened?"

"I got up late this morning, mom. Anyway, you know I wasn't going to miss seeing you this weekend, since tomorrow, Sunday, May 11th will be your special day, Mother's Day."

"And I'm going to cook for you the fattest rooster in the yard. I am so happy to see you. By the way, your sister Ivy is coming here tomorrow and the whole family will be here. That will be my best Mother's Day present."

And it was truly a splendid Mother's Day with all his siblings and their families and his parents together again and they were all so very happy.

Suddenly, though, his thoughts turned to Lisa. She must be at her relative with her mother celebrating this day with them. He couldn't wait to see her the next weekend when he planned to stay over in Colon. He thought to himself that he had to stop putting off the day when he would introduce Lisa to his parents. That day will certainly be in July, when Lisa is on vacation.

On returning to Silver City after Mother's Day, a lot of things were going to change. He was certainly not going to any more parties without Lisa; and he was not going to get involved again with Iona and her mother after the treachery they and their co-conspirator friends had pulled. He told no one about what had happened that night, and he decided not to think about it anymore.

The following Saturday, May 17th, when he saw Lisa and went out with her in the evening, there was a lot to talk about since they hadn't been together for more than a week, including the previous weekend, and that was a long time since their relationship started to grow stronger.

"Did you pray every night as we promised?" she asked him.

"Why, of course," he replied, but he was lying for that night when he was at the party drunk and later with Iona, treachery or not, he did no such thing. "Did you?" He posed the same question to her.

"Of course, I prayed every night at 11:30 p.m. as we pledged to do. What did you do during the time since I last saw you? By the way, how was your friend's engagement party?"

"O, it was alright, but I was glad when it was over since you weren't there. The rest of the time when we were apart, I was very lonely. What about you? How did you manage? How are your relatives?"

Everyone is fine, thank you; but I feel like something between us is different somehow. I missed you during these past twelve days."

Then they embraced and kissed and somehow the chemistry was still there. He explained to her that in the summer they would make up for lost time, and that filled her with the reassurance that she needed.

In no time the end of the school year arrived, Thursday, May 29, 1952. Grades were given out; all of his students were promoted, and the teachers got together for an informal farewell office party. They gathered in an empty classroom across from the principal's office after early dismissal, and, after turning in their books and unused supplies, they enjoyed some light refreshments and tasty "bocadillos" as they talked and discussed their plans for the summer.

"I know everybody is going to attend summer school next week at La Boca High," said Rudolph Barnes. "How about you, Darryl, are you attending?"

"We'd be fools not to," said Darryl, "I understand we will get college credits through the Balboa Jr. College Extension that can be applied toward an advanced degree."

"That means a chance to get on the U. S. pay scale as Johnson promised us," said Ronald Wilson.

"How does that work now?" asked Daisy Biggett.

"Johnson promised that if we got the equivalent of a bachelor's degree or higher, he would place us on the pay scale equivalent to Washington, D. C. teachers which is a U. S. rate," responded Ronald.

"You cannot get a B.A. degree from the Jr. College Extension," said Darryl. "I understand that you can only get credits for an A.A. certificate that way."

"And what's wrong with that?" asked Rudolph Barnes.

"Nothing," said Darryl, "in fact next summer you can take the A.A. certificate along with a transcript to Nebraska University, for example, and finish up in less than 8 weeks for the B.A."

"A lot of teachers are doing that already," said Daisy.

"That's right, some of them are going to Nebraska this summer to finish up," added Ronald.

"Yeah, thanks to Lawrence Johnson for the opportunity to get a decent pay in this Canal Zone school system," interjected James.

"I guess that settles the question then," said Rudolph who brought the subject up in the first place, and he turned to the room full of fellow teachers and asked the question one more time.

"Who is going to the summer school next week in La Boca?"

They all raised their hands in unison and said how they were looking forward to seeing each other in La Boca. Just then principal Weakley entered the room and, after getting their attention, made a toast with a glass of lemonade.

"It has been a very good year. I have enjoyed working with all of you, and I am proud of you. I wish you a very good summer school and a wonderful summer vacation."

And they all responded in unison with glasses raised.

"Thanks Weakley; we love you, too!"

And Weakley didn't forget to remind them of one more thing.

"Before I forget, I hope you all will be kind enough to clean up this mess and turn in all your books and keys and don't forget to sign your release forms before you leave."

And within another hour or so, everyone had departed, leaving Weakley and a couple trusted workers behind to close the school building.

After leaving the elementary school that Thursday evening, James went home to pack because the next day, Friday, May 30th would be Memorial Day, and on Sunday he will be returning to Panama. On Saturday he met Lisa after work, and they spent some time together. They talked about the summer and how difficult it was going to be not seeing each other every week during the coming month. They agreed to meet near the end of summer school to plan a vacation together in July, before the new school year began. He took the noon train for Panama City.

Now that school vacation had come, he focused on attending the four-week teacher-training summer school at La Boca High School. He was looking forward to attending classes, and, when he was not in class, helping around the house in Parque LeFevre or working out at the gym with his brother and other gymnasts.

Chapter XIII:

The Mysterious Letter from the

Superintendent's Office

Lisa was looking forward to her first vacation from her job in the latter part of July and James was planning to ask her at that time to be his bride. Yes, that would be a good time, he thought, for them to take that step when they both would be on vacation together. But the whole world suddenly turned upside down on July 3, 1952 when a letter dated Friday, June 30, 1952 marked 'Special Delivery' arrived at his parents' home addressed to him from the Office of the Superintendent of Schools. He couldn't imagine for what reason he was receiving such a letter. He was more surprised than curious as he opened it.

OFFICE OF THE SUPERINTENDENT OF SCHOOLS
BALBOA HEIGHTS, CANAL ZONE

June 30, 1952

Dear James Edwards:

You are requested to report to the Office of the Superintendent of Schools on Monday, July 7, 1952, at 10 a.m. for an important meeting. It is urgent that you attend this meeting. If you are unable to attend please contact this office immediately with an explanation in order to re-schedule.

> *Respectfully,*
>
> *Supervisor of Instruction,*
>
> *Alfred E. Osborne*
>
> *Office of the Superintendent*
>
> *Balboa Heights, C. Z.*

Now he was more than curious. Since the letter gave no clue, he did not know what to make of it. Why was he being summoned to a meeting in the Superintendent's office? This was a quandary for which he had no explanation.

On Monday morning, July 7, 1952, when he arrived at the superintendent's office, to his amazement he saw Sephora Reid sitting there and she had brought a lawyer with her. Also present were the Superintendent, the Supervisor of Instruction and a secretary taking notes. After greeting and introducing everyone, the Supervisor of Instruction opened the meeting by establishing that the persons present, meaning Sephora Reid and James Edwards, were acquainted with each other. James wished that it were not so! The Supervisor then held a legal letter of complaint in his hand and without reading it aloud summarized its contents as he addressed James directly.

"Mistress Sephora Reid charges that you, James Edwards, are responsible for her daughter, Iona Reid, becoming pregnant. She is two months with child and Mrs. Reid says she has proof that you had sex with her daughter on the night of May 9, 1952 thereby causing her to be pregnant. Do you have anything to say regarding these charges?"

He paused, waiting for an answer from James. James was trying hard to restrain the emotions he was feeling. He sat there weighing the gravity of the situation, and what it meant. His world was being shattered. His teaching career was in jeopardy. What would he do if he should lose his position? What choices does a young colored man in the Panama Canal Zone have, anyway, when he reaches adulthood? First of all, in the Canal Zone there is no Civil Rights for blacks, no due process, no teachers union to protect them or fight for them, so there is no job security. And when it comes to job opportunities, if you are lucky, you might find unskilled work in the commissaries or the clubhouses, perhaps, or get a job as a helper or a servant. But you could never aspire to being a professional such as a doctor, lawyer, supervisor, engineer, pilot, chemist, nurse, etc. Neither could you seek a career in Panama without mastery of the Spanish language -- which James did not have, growing up in the Panama Canal Zone. Therefore, the only profession available that he could train for was that of a schoolteacher. And now, if they should take that away from him, he is finished! What would he do? James sat there frustrated, full of anger, for the cruel and unfair circumstance he now found himself in as the Supervisor of Instruction's words seeped into his brain, and he remembered that night that brought this situation about that threatened his career.

"I have only one question for Mrs. Reid," James replied, turning toward her: "As Iona's parent, why didn't you contact my parents rather than bring these charges against me to my employer? You know that your daughter and I were never in a relationship. We were never dating each other at any time and there was nothing between us; in fact, it was only the last-minute pleading by the hostess, Jean, that made me agree to escort your daughter to the party on the night of May 9, 1952, and she is just as responsible, or even more responsible, for what happened."

As she fidgeted in her chair everyone was waiting for her answer.

"Well...I...I heard things," she said, "I heard that he was going to do the same thing that the first one did who lied and abandoned my daughter. If I didn't have proof I swear that is what he was going to do -- use my daughter and make her pregnant and then walk away to leave her parents to carry the burden. I knew that by coming here first before I took it to the courts and to the newspapers that the school was going to protect its reputation. I am sure that's not the kind of teacher you want the public to know you hire to teach in your schools."

It was no use, she acted like she didn't even hear a word that James said and went on with her accusation. She knew very well the position that this would put the school system in because they did not want any uncalled for scrutiny and publicity and they were sensitive to any kind of scandal that would be publicized in the newspapers about the way they were running the colored schools, so she had them at her mercy. Still, she didn't answer the question, why didn't she contact James or his parents and inform them about the situation first before going to the school administration. Apparently It was not her intention to do that, but, rather, it was her intention to try to force the school's hand and get her way.

The administration didn't care a biscuit about the personal issues between the two families nor who was dishonest to whom. Their bottom line was protecting the reputation of their Canal Zone colored schools and keeping their name out of a scandal in the local newspapers at all costs. There was a threat to go to the newspapers and to the courts. That was their only concern. And since James couldn't prove he was not responsible, they gave him an ultimatum.

"Either you marry this young lady and father her child when she gives birth, or else you can no longer work in the Canal Zone Schools. As of this moment, therefore, your employment is suspended until you can provide us with proof that you have complied with this decision and it is confirmed by Mrs. Reid; then you will be reinstated without prejudice and reassigned to another school."

Fair or unfair, just or unjust, if he didn't comply, this would mean the end of his teaching career, as well as his means of earning a living, and the end of everything he had been working towards. His parents and family would be devastated because they are the ones who invested the most in him. They invested what little resources they had, besides their love and care, so he could become the first one in the family with a good education and a profession. They could just take that away like that and ruin his reputation on the word of one individual. A million things were going through his brain at that moment. He was devastated! It was a little too much for a young man just starting out in life to bear.

They gave him until the end of July to make a decision and to inform them of it, that is, either comply with their demand and become reinstated to his teaching position, or else decline to comply and be permanently expelled with no future in the Canal Zone school system or on the Canal Zone and with a letter placed in his personnel file disparaging his character. Of course, even if he refused to comply he would still have a paternity court case to deal with and, without a job, the burden would fall on his family. There was no way he could win in this situation. Looks like Sephora had snared him well and Iona's chances of getting a husband were looking good after all.

When he returned home and told his family what had happened and the alternatives confronting him, after the first wave of shock that he had gotten himself into such a predicament wore off, they gave him their complete and whole-hearted support no matter what he decided to do. Of course they were very upset at the way he was treated like a criminal, as if he had not been brought up the right way to face up to his responsibilities. They questioned, too, whether the girl was truthful and whether it could have been someone else, but he, their son, could not give them that assurance when he explained how he was seduced and was in no position to rule out the possibility that he was responsible. In those days there was no fool-proof scientific way of proving paternity (DNA tests had not yet been developed as infallible proof of paternity) and all the authorities needed was the girl's declaration and with that, combined with the evidence of his complicity, seduced or not, there was no way he could win. That night he agonized about what to do and hardly got any sleep.

The next day, Tuesday, July 8th his sister, Ivy, came by the home and when James told her everything she was not happy at all.

"You mean you are going to let that woman get away with this after the way she treated you? And why do you let her put this pregnancy on you? Her daughter is an experienced woman who is older than you with a child already out of wedlock and she has had other men in her life. Why did they do this to my brother?"

Her father tried to calm her down and explained to her:

"Your brother knew her and she claimed he had sex with her. She named him as the one responsible and he can't prove otherwise. They have all the cards and they have no intention of letting him go. So calm down, daughter, and let's see how we can help your brother."

"I didn't mean to get angry. I am sorry. I knew something like this was going to happen when he went to that town with no family to look after him. So what have you decided to do?"

"Under the circumstances," said James, "I have to accept responsibility for the child, and I will lose my job if I do not marry her. I can't give up my career; I can't do that!"

"And you can't marry someone you don't love either," said his sister. "This is a forced marriage; there is only one thing to do."

"And that is?" asked Mr. Edwards, Sr.

"Consult a lawyer."

"You said she brought a lawyer with her to the meeting, right son?" asked his father.

"Yes."

"Then your sister is right. A lawyer will tell us what to do."

"And I know just the right lawyer that we need," said Ivy. "I am going to call him right now and make an appointment."

On Wednesday, July 9th, James and his sister went to see David De Leon, one of the best divorce lawyers in Panama. It helped a great deal to know that the attorney's wife and James's sister, Ivy, were good friends.

"Hello Ivy, come in. It's good to see you again, how is Bertrand?"

"He is fine. He's doing better than me right now."

"How is that, Ivy?"

"David, meet my brother James."

"How are you James? I am glad to meet you."

"I am glad to meet you, too, sir," replied James.

"My brother is in a bad situation," said Ivy, "and I hope that you will be able to tell us what to do. We need some legal advice."

"I am sure I'll be able to help you, please explain."

"Since he graduated from the La Boca Normal school he has been teaching in Silver City, Colon, going on about three years now. He came home this June for summer vacation and while he was home he received a letter from the Superintendent of Schools summoning him to a meeting in his office. To his astonishment there was this woman, a Mrs. Reid from Silver City, who went to the administration and accused my brother like a common criminal of making her daughter pregnant and she wanted them to do something about it since he works in their schools. She did this before telling his parents or him anything. She and her daughter, and a group of lady friends, entrapped and seduced my brother one night and if I am not mistaken drugged him and compromised him so that he can't even remember clearly what happened. The superintendent gave him an ultimatum to either marry her or permanently lose his teaching position. This doesn't seem fair in any way, shape or form."

"I know how you feel, Ivy, but from a legal standpoint if they can prove that he had sex with her no matter the circumstances, since she named him as the one responsible, I am afraid he is stuck with the paternity. However, where marriage is concerned, he doesn't have to marry her but they can fire him from his job for not marrying her if that is their policy. It's the Canal Zone; you know there's no black teacher's union, no civil rights, no colored people rights, and they can do anything they want to us, you know that."

"Then that means he has to marry her to keep his job?"

"In a way, yes, but there is a solution. He doesn't have to stay married. In fact, all he has to do is sign the piece of paper in a Canal Zone civil court that says he is married and the marriage can be annulled in the Panamanian courts as long as the marriage is not consummated. Do you understand what I mean?"

"I am not sure I do."

"As long as they do not live together as husband and wife then the marriage is not consummated, and it therefore can be annulled in Panama."

"I understand what you mean. They are married in name only, but no sexual contact after the marriage."

"Right, now James, and this is for you. If you marry her you must not have sex with her after the marriage, or to put it more succinctly, you must not live together as husband and wife. Then the divorce is a simple formality. In fact I will handle it for you myself for a nominal fee."

With this information James decided to comply with the superintendent's ultimatum and he contacted Mrs. Reid that same evening to offer to schedule a meeting between her and his parents.

Sephora was only too happy to come to such a meeting for to her it meant that she had won and this was exactly the outcome that she wanted. The two families met on Saturday, 7-12-1952 at 2 p.m. at the Edwards home in Parque LeFevre, Panama. The meeting was very restrained but cordial as Mr. and

Mrs. Edwards were not very happy about it but went along with the decision their son had made to keep his job.

Six days later on Friday morning, 7-18-1952, a civil marriage between Iona and James took place in Balboa, C.Z. magistrate court with Mr. Edwards and Mrs. Reid as witnesses. Afterwards, they had a brief meeting and the two sides came to an understanding. Iona returned to Silver City and James to Parque LeFevre to stay with their respective parents until such time as other arrangements could be made. The C.Z. school administration was given proof which Mrs. Reid confirmed and James Edwards was reinstated to a teaching position though he was not returned to Silver City but transferred to La Boca Elementary School to start the new school year. During that same year, attorney De Leon filed for divorce in the 1st Circuit Court of Panama.

Chapter XIV:

A Heavy Price to Pay

James was in a state of derangement for some time and found it hard to accept what had happened. He was very depressed and felt as if he were in a nightmare that he would soon awaken from. However, it was no nightmare. What happened was real, and, after the marriage, his attorney strongly advised him not to go to Colon while the divorce case was in progress. That left him with only one alternative. He wrote Lisa a letter.

In the letter he explained to her his predicament, and what had happened, how it happened, how he was used, heavily drugged, was seduced, during and after the party, 'till his judgment was clouded and impaired. He still took responsibility, however, for his part, and he hated himself for letting his guard down that night. He poured out his heart and asked her to forgive him, and if she did, he promised they would be together again. He told her how much he loved her and always will, that he was seeking an annulment of the marriage that never should have taken place. If she were to leave him, though, he would understand and would never blame her for it, but he wanted her to know that he would never stop loving her.

He mailed the letter on July 19, 1952, to her home address in Silver City Heights, hoping that she would receive it before their next scheduled meeting that they had set for Friday, July 25, 1952.

Lisa, in the meantime, was anxiously waiting to hear from him and to take the next step as they had agreed to do. July 25th came and went and, not hearing from him, she began to sense that something terrible had happened and she was frantic. There was no way she could contact him by phone, since her parents didn't have a telephone in their home (not many in the West Indian community had a home phone in those days), and she didn't know his home phone number, if he had one; nevertheless, she trusted James and she knew that, somehow, he would get in touch with her and then everything would be as it should be. So, she waited a few more days, but it was getting close to the end of summer vacation and in Silver City, such a small town where news is concerned, gossip spreads easily and the news was finally brought to her attention. She was distraught and could not believe it. **James had married someone else!** How could that be? How could this have happened? No, it was impossible!

"Lisa," said her sister Naomi, "you hear how these women are carrying on about your boyfriend, James;

it's terrible! Why don't you call him, or go and see him and find out for yourself what is going on?"

"No," said Lisa, "I will not do that. He made a promise to me and if what they are saying is true, he is not who I thought he was, and I will never see him again. And if it is not true, then it's up to him to do something about it and show me that he really loves me, and that this is some kind of mistake. O sis, James does not love me! If it was all a lie, and he really doesn't love me, then I don't want him either!"

She was being hard because she was hurting inside; she really wanted desperately to see him but not under these circumstances. He would have to be the one to communicate to her, somehow, and convince her that this is just a nightmare; that this is not happening and tell her to her face that this is not true. In the meantime, she would at least wait until the school year started again in a couple of weeks before she did anything. When August came and school was reopened, she waited until the week of August 11th when she decided that if he ever had any intention of contacting her, or seeing her again, he would have done so already. She stayed home from work on Thursday and Friday, August 14th, and 15th, and on Thursday morning she called Silver City Elementary School from a public phone.

"Is this Silver City Elementary School?"

"Yes, it is."

The person on the other end was principal Weakley.

"May I please speak to Mr. James Edwards, sir?"

"I am afraid you will not be able to do so, ma'am."

"Why, may I ask?"

"He no longer works here. I believe he is now teaching in La Boca Elementary School. You'll have to call there to speak to him."

"Thank you, sir." And she hung up.

Now, there was absolutely no doubt in her mind. She had dreaded all along that it must be true, that she had lost her first true love that she once thought was made in Heaven. And since he would not come to her, and she had not heard from him, she would finally go to La Boca Elementary School and confront him in person.

Her sister, Naomi, accompanied her from Silver City on Friday morning, August 15th, and they went to the school where James worked. It was just about noon when they arrived at La Boca Elementary School that had already dismissed classes for lunch break. They stopped at the principal's office.

"Could you direct us to Mr. James Edwards' classroom, please?"

"Yes," said the secretary, "his classroom is upstairs on the second floor, the 3rd one on the left facing the playground. He usually has his lunch alone in his classroom."

He was sitting behind his desk about to finish a sandwich during lunchtime, at approximately 12:10 p.m., when he heard the knock on his door; and just as he opened the door and saw her standing there, his heartbeat accelerated and he was filled with unspeakable joy, and agony, at the same time.

"Lisa...," he said, his heart pounding, his mind praying for a miracle, his lips fumbling for words, "come...come in..."

She gracefully entered and she never looked more beautiful, although there was a deep sadness and hurt written on her face. He tried to offer her a seat, but she refused to sit.

"Is it true what they say...?" she pleaded... "tell me, is it true...? And tears welled up in her eyes and streamed down her beautiful face.

He wanted to hold her, to hug her, to reassure her, to tell her how much he loved her, to tell her a different story that would end this horror he was experiencing … but he could not. He could not undo what had been done.

"I... I... am sorry... Lisa." Those were the only words that managed to come out of his mouth, "...I... I... am sorry."

And before he could do anything else, or say another word, she said, "Goodbye," and quickly turned and ran out of the room, through the hallway and down the stairs, her sister close behind her.

He watched her from an open window in his classroom as she hurriedly walked away in the distance, and how he tried to hold back the tears that inside his heart were tearing him apart as he felt like dying for the first time in his young life. He stood there for some time gazing into the distance long after she had disappeared, and wondered how this could have happened to him, how he could have arrived at such a moment in his life, how it could be that he had found his true love and then lost her, and he tried to hold back the silent tears. If only things had been different!

A year later seemed like a lifetime, and each passing day he was haunted by the memory of that last meeting as he relived the details of it. Yet, despite everything that had happened, he was still clinging to the hope that he would be able to win her back after all the hurt, the anger and enough time had passed, and after his unfortunate false marriage was dissolved. Certainly, if he had the chance, he thought, he would prove to her that he had not betrayed their love; that he loved her still and always will. What lover would not forgive another knowing that he was wronged and that his heart was still true to her?

He recalls that, during the months following their separation, he had pressed Attorney De Leon many times for news about the annulment, even though he knew how hard he was working on it. Finally, after a little over a year had passed, De Leon was successful in getting the case resolved before the 1st circuit court in Panama City, and, in August 1954, the marriage was finally dissolved. Arrangements were made through the court for child support and James' family agreed to help. He never saw Sephora Reid again, nor any of her co-conspirator friends. Lisa, though, was constantly on his mind, and, when he became legally free from the marriage, he was eager to find her again and to reconcile with her. What he did not know at the time, however, was that Lisa had given her hand to another suitor. Although James had won her heart, when she walked away from him hurt that day, August 15, 1952, she returned to Silver City and not long thereafter accepted from another suitor an offer of marriage that was speedily consummated. Even if this suitor could not make her as happy as James could, she did not care, she told her sister, at least he could never break her heart the way that James had done. So, when his marriage was dissolved and he came around inquiring about Lisa, he was told that she had married and no longer lived there, that he should forget about her and should go on with his life just as she had done with hers. As always, his family was there to support him and they did not like to see him brooding and sad, and reminded him that he had an ambition once to go abroad and study and further his education, that studies and a change of venue were what he needed; so, two and a half years later, his sister, who had preceded him to the U.S., arranged for him to come and live with her and her husband in Brooklyn, N.Y. until he found a place of his own.

Chapter XV:

Brooklyn, New York, June 9, 1956

On arriving in Brooklyn, N.Y. on June 9, 1956, James took up residence with his sister and her husband, and, for a few years, tried selling stocks and bonds and mutual funds for a living. He soon decided that that career was not for him, that he was meant to be a schoolteacher, not a salesman, so he enrolled in Brooklyn College on a tuition-free scholarship, attending first part-time at night, then in his last year, full time in the day while doing odd jobs to help pay for his incidental expenses. By 1966 he had completed his B.A. degree at Brooklyn College, taken a full-time teaching position in the New York City public schools and moved into his own apartment in Brooklyn. In the ensuing years while teaching in New York City school system, he attended City College Graduate School where he earned two master's degrees and was promoted to Associate Director of a secondary school in New York City, doing some writing in his spare time.

Attending undergraduate and graduate schools had kept him busy and his mind was occupied most of the time with his studies and his career, but, in the late 1960's, he was active again socially, going to parties and meeting new friends. He was active, yet, despite subsequent romantic affairs, even a second marriage that eventually failed, he never found a love that could replace Lisa. Other female interests came into his life, but it was no use. If those efforts were successful, he might have stopped thinking about her. It was such a long time ago, almost a lifetime, and although he had tried very hard many times to forget her, he could not.

One day in the spring of 1982 while reminiscing about the past, the events of August 15, 1952, came back to him and with it a thought that troubled him. In their last meeting, (perhaps due to the highly emotional state they were both in at the time), neither he nor Lisa had mentioned anything about the letter he had written her the day after the forced civil marriage in Balboa Magistrate Court took place, which ended their relationship. Would that letter have made a difference, anyway, he now wondered. He had hoped it would. He had mailed it on July 19, 1952, hoping that she would receive it before the 25th when they had planned to meet. You would think that after thirty years had passed that such details would not come back to haunt him! He had tried to settle the past in his mind by assuming that on August 15, 1952 when they last saw each other, that she had read his letter, and had dismissed it, as well as his sentiments.

But, somehow, that thought never fully satisfied him. Now, he had so much doubt about that theory that, as he reflected on the Lisa he once knew and loved, in his heart and mind it was impossible to see how such a flawed theory could be true. He asked himself the question, "Then why was there no mention of, or response to, my letter at the time or any time after?" Then it occurred to him, that maybe she never received his letter in the first place! What if the letter was intercepted by someone else at the time, or was misplaced in someone else's mail by error? What if, somehow, it had gotten lost in the mail? He had not thought about these possibilities in the years past, but now he realized that such things have been known to happen. Sometimes undelivered letters are thrown into a "dead letter file" and are never seen again. Sometimes letters get lost in the postal system for years until they show up mysteriously. There have been cases of letters mailed but never reached their intended destinations. In one such case he had recently read about, in the U.S. in Chicago, Illinois, in the year 1941, a letter, which was mailed by a serviceman to his loved one, was finally delivered to its intended address 40 years after it was mailed. Unfortunately, by the time it arrived at its intended address, his sweetheart had been long gone. What a terrible twist of fate that would have been had that happened in his case! Now, he will never know the answer.

On Lisa's part, the years, too, didn't just vanish without her own share of remembrances and misgivings. After all, she is human, too, and since she was once in love with James, and they had shared intimate moments together, she, too, could not dismiss the past so easily, and must have grappled with it, and with the question in her heart and mind, "What if he really loved her?" As time passed, and she heard the real story from her close friends, about the conspiracy, the unfair accusations presented to the school, the ultimatum, the false marriage, the divorce, etcetera, she must have come to the realization that something very wrong had happened in the past, and that James had to have been terribly compromised before he would jeopardize what the two of them had together, and that it was a marriage he was forced into against his will. If only today was thirty years ago, she thought to herself, she might not have run away and judged him wrongfully. It is too late now for regrets, but at least she still has memories and the little love poem he once gave her in Colon. She will keep that forever.

Chapter XVI:

Reconnecting with Panamanian-West Indian Roots

James was not the only Panamanian emigrant who left Panama to come to the U.S. to live. As a matter of fact, when the 1955 Remon-Eisenhower treaty went into effect, the handwriting was already on the wall foretelling the liquidation of the United States Canal Zone that would precipitate a 1950's, 1960's and 1970's exodus of Panamanian-West Indians from Panama to the United States. Twenty-two years after the signing of the 1955 Remon- Eisenhower treaty, the 1977 Torrijos-Carter treaty sealed the coffin of the final Canal Zone liquidation. With emigration, Panamanian-West Indians took with them all of their popular clubs and organizations from Panama as they re-established themselves in the United States. Brooklyn, especially, seemed at one time to be a colony of Panamanian expatriates where Panamanian social, cultural and political events were occurring regularly in various quarters, especially in the Bedford-Stuyvesant and Kings County regions.

After the famous Conference of Panamanians took place in the Poconos in 1974, a group of Panamanians met in Brooklyn to share recollections about past experiences of an era that is almost forgotten, an era that current descendants of Panamanian West Indians know very little about. This group of expatriates was persistent in pursuing the subject of their heritage, and James remembered, when he received an invitation to join them in one of their informal meetings, how stimulating and heated the discussions were. This was in 1981 and in that same year, as "Friends of George Westerman," they undertook to introduce and promote the publication of Westerman's book, "Los Inmigrantes Antillanos en Panama" (The West Indian Immigrants in Panama), by hosting a "book party" at the Restoration Center, Brooklyn, N.Y. with the evening highlighted by a dramatic skit that relived a past Canal Zone West Indian domestic scene. It was a great success!

The seed that was planted then, for the study and preservation of West Indian heritage and contributions to Panama, grew stronger and the following April, 1982, a group of "Concerned Friends" gave a testimonial dinner in the Number One Restaurant in Chinatown, New York City to honor two of the most famous pioneers of their Isthmian past, Dr. George Westerman and the Reverend Dr. Ephraim Alphonse. At the mid-point of the program a suspicious fire broke out in the kitchen of the Chinese restaurant and they heard some frantic Chinese mumbo jumbo coming from the kitchen. Thanks to a Chinese interpreter who was sitting in the audience who translated the urgency into English to mean "FIRE" and "EVACUATE," everyone became aware of the danger. Fortunately, all hearts kept calm and the entire audience very safely and orderly evacuated from the premises. Providence stepped in and all the guests were safely transported from Chinatown to 276 Lafayette Ave., Brooklyn, N.Y., the home of their famous matriarch, Mrs. Anesta Samuel and her devoted husband, Mr. Henry Samuel. There, at the home of the Samuels that evening the program continued and, in their garden, a special ceremony was conducted in which the "ancestral torch" was symbolically handed down from the two distinguished elders to their succeeding generation, represented by Ms. Melba Lowe and Dr. Maurice Heywood.

After this, the desire to do more to honor their ancestors was so great that the next time they met, at the home of Henry and Anesta Samuels in Brooklyn, they decided then and there to set about forming the organization that came to be known as: (PWIHA) Panamanian-West Indian Heritage Association. A constitution was soon written and ratified, officers elected and sworn in, and the organization was officially incorporated in New York State and set out on its chartered course: "Dedication to the research, preservation and dissemination of the history, culture, heritage of Panamanians of Afro-West Indian descent and their contributions to the Republic of Panama, as well as to the world."

In the years that followed, between 1982 and the first decade of the second millennium, that organization had created a very impressive record of accomplishments during its twenty-plus years of existence, and, in that time period in addition to establishing, celebrating and sponsoring numerous events, public forums, conferences, films, tributes, programs, honoring West Indian pioneers and pillars of former Panamanian-West Indian communities, they sponsored "Diggers," a film researched and produced by Roman Foster, "Women of Courage," a program dedicated to pioneer Panama Canal Zone West Indian women, "Torchbearers to Glory 1925-1955," a program honoring past Panamanian-West Indian athletes, and other programs honoring past Canal Zone West Indian community leaders, elders, preachers, and educators. They published journals, brochures, and photo albums put together from mementos and photographs submitted by members of the Panamanian West Indian diaspora from all corners, in response to mailing inquiries and a call to lend pictures and articles and artifacts. They also contributed, significantly, articles and financial support to the (SAMAAP), the Society of Friends of the African-West Indian Museum in Panama.

By the time the first decade of the 21st century had ended, unfortunately, the organization that started out with so much promise and vitality began to decline, and eventually faded out of existence. Most of its founding members passed away, some left New York for other states, and only a very few remained in Brooklyn.

As an epilogue to that era of the PWIHA organization, an old friend said to James not long ago:

"You know, we may be the last vestige of the "silver people" with first-hand knowledge of life as it used to be in the old "silver towns" of La Boca, Paraiso, Red Tank, Gamboa (Santa Cruz), Gatun, Silver City, etc., where West Indians once lived in the Panama Canal Zone. After our generations are gone, there will be no one left to tell the story of **our forgotten people**." He could only agree without further comment.

Apart from the foregoing PWIHA and its history, several other Panamanian-West Indian organizations and groups flourished during the peak years of resettlement of immigrant Panamanian-West Indians in Brooklyn and other New York City neighborhoods.

With the exception of a few, such as the Panama Canal International Alumni Association, The Dedicators, Inc., and the La Boca Alumni Assn. (Club El Pacifico), hardly any of them still exist today. During the peak years, 1950's – 2000, on many occasions different Panamanian groups, either separately or jointly, besides celebrating independence day (3rd of November) with parades in Brooklyn every year, would hold social events, political events, public forums and panel discussions on various topics of common interest to Panamanian West Indians living abroad. There was always a gathering taking place somewhere.

On one occasion that made a lasting impression on James, a public forum was organized at a venue in Brooklyn, N.Y. with a slate of panelists and experts that dealt with the subject of "The Plight of West Indians in the Panama Canal Zone and the Role of Panamanian Nationalism and its Impact on the West Indian community."

The panelists were Panamanian West Indian experts who had studied and written a great deal about the subject. Restated another way the topic of the discussion was:

"THE ROLE OF THE PANAMANIAN GOVERNMENT IN THE WEST INDIAN STRUGGLE FOR JUSTICE IN PANAMA AND THE CANAL ZONE; AND

PANAMANIAN NATIONALISM AND ITS CONTRIBUTION TO THE DECLINE OF WEST INDIAN CULTURE IN PANAMA."

"First of all," said panelist no.1, "The Panamanian government that existed in the early years, after the birth of the republic, couldn't even help itself much less help West Indians. During the first decades of its occupation by the U.S., Panama presented no kind of resistance or aggressiveness toward the United States of America, and even came to regard West Indians, at one time, as undesirable aliens in their country. It wasn't until after they matured and found out that they, too, were an illegitimate offspring of the same United States that birthed them, and that they, too, were being screwed over, just like the West Indians, by the same "Yankees," that they even began to question or challenge them in any way."

"What do you mean?" asked a member of the audience.

"Just this: that Panama was born under the wings of the liberating arms of the U. S. who freed them from Columbia (with U.S. gunboat diplomacy[25] threatening Columbian forces if they dared to cross the border, and with U.S. dollars buying off Columbian soldiers to give up the fight) and made it possible for them to become a Panamanian nation; so they were beholden to the "gringos" and had a growing-up process to go through first before they had enough "cojones" (audacity) to even challenge American authority and policies in Panama --- in fact, the first U.S.-Panama treaty (1903) was a swindle and a Frenchman, not a Panamanian, signed it representing Panama."

"Meaning," said panelist no. 2, "for decades, starting from 1904, the U. S. had practically the whole Isthmus to themselves to do whatever they wanted and they even considered the Canal Zone as United States territory and Panama and the Canal as part of their empire. Meanwhile the then newborn Panamanian government was too weak politically and militarily to do anything and too dependent on U. S. money (Yankee dollar), power and influence so they never officially did or could interfere with whatever the Americans were doing in their country at that time."

A person in the audience asked the question, "How did West Indians defend themselves against the injustices in the Canal Zone if there was no one to defend them against the tyranny of the Canal Zone bigots and racists? It is known that even the British government had abandoned them."

"Yes, that is true. The British gave some token aide to the first West Indians (British subjects) but afterwards they abandoned their descendants and left them to their own fates. But I'll try to answer the question another way," said panelist #2, "and you'll see what resilience and fortitude West Indian descendants possessed who took up the struggle with or without any outside help:

During the construction of the Canal and since it was built, our grandfathers and fathers suffered for decades at the hands of the white man under the cursed "gold and silver" standard with little or no help from a Panamanian government that didn't want us in their country anyway, a British government that abandoned us, and a U.S. government in Washington that allowed local U.S. racist elements to establish and maintain a white utopia in the Panama Canal Zone until the 1st and 2nd generation West Indians grew up there and became tired of seeing their parents oppressed, belittled, humiliated, underpaid, and treated like lower class members of society. The early West Indian workers had taken a stand on their own once, in 1920[26], seeking improvements in wages, in better living conditions and better treatment and they paid dearly for it with the loss of jobs, demotions, and reductions in their already measly pay, and in some cases they were blackballed from the Isthmus. It took 20 more years, by which time the world had changed, and a younger breed of West

Indians dared to stand up to the tyrants. They could no longer hold on to their little white Utopia, their tight-knit cabal in their white privilege enclave that they kept to themselves and defended fiercely against all who threatened it. The screws first started coming apart, though, when (a) In 1943 a protest group of Colon West Indians wrote a denunciation[27] of the Panama Canal Company's treatment of West Indians entitled "A Forgotten People" in which was detailed numerous grievances and was circulated in a pamphlet to the Anglo-American Caribbean Commission that was meeting that same year in Washington, D.C. The U.S. Chair of the Commission, Charles Tausig, had the complaints investigated and submitted a report lambasting racial policies of the Canal Zone. (b) In 1944 a Panamanian delegation, including labor representatives, attended an International Labor Organization Conference in Philadelphia[28] and embarrassed the United States by presenting to the U.S. Labor Secretary Francis Perkins a memorial to the discrimination against Panamanian-West Indian employees on the Canal Zone; (c) In 1944 Panamanian-West Indian Leaders in Panama held a mass meeting[29] and collected over 5,000 signatures on a petition requesting urgent action on a list of grievances that had been presented to Vice-President Henry Wallace the year before, (1943), for the improvement of silver workers' conditions, for providing benefits for retired and laid-off silver employees, for providing newer and improved living quarters, and allowing freer movement to and from the U. S.; (d) In 1945 the Colored Teachers Association (CTA) joined with the Panama Canal West Indian Employees Association (PCWIEA) and succeeded in getting the U.S. Secretary of War, H. L. Stimson, to grant local 713 branch of the CIO the rights to bargain as a Panamanian labor Union instead of as a Local Rate Union, which would give it more teeth in keeping with the 1936 Hull-Alfaro treaty[30] as spelled out in Cordell Hull's note of 1936 in the treaty that called for equal employment practices between U.S. and Panamanian citizens; and Governor Mehaffey had to go along with it out of fear that a more militant Mexican labor boss (Lombardo Toledano) waiting in the wings would be much worse if he moved into the vacuum created and unionized all Panamanians as an alternative. Local 713 Under Gaskin as its president published a newspaper, the "ac-CIO-n" denouncing zone practices; and (e) In 1948 an expose on the conditions in the Panama Canal Zone was written by George Westerman in the U. S. magazine "Common Ground" which also found its way to U. S. legislators and high officials. All of these listed elements initiated by West Indians themselves, along with the help of the Workman and the Tribune (West Indian publications) speaking out for them helped to precipitate a wave of investigations and subsequent actions to pressure the white Zonians to change the Canal Zone system.

From investigations several reports and recommendations were submitted: one by Commissioner Tausig, one by the Department of Defense, one by the Labor Secretary Perkins, and one by General McSherry to President Truman, all recommending an overhauling of the personnel policies and practices in the Canal Zone to correct the gross inequalities."

"Didn't President Roosevelt or Truman do anything about the complaints and recommendations that their officials submitted?" someone in the audience asked.

Panelist #1 jumped in:

"I'll answer that question. Of course Truman did or tried to do something. When you consider that in those days right after WWII the communist threat was making everybody nervous, Truman himself was fearful that the situation on the Canal Zone could be ripe for Communist influence; so when the reports came to him that the Personnel Department on the Zone was dominated by the MTC/CLU (Metal Trade Council/Central Labor Union) and they were determined to preserve white supremacy and white privilege through blatant racial discrimination practices in the Canal Zone, and President Truman's officers recommended to him the dismantling of the "Gold" & "Silver" designations and replacing the gold/silver payroll system with a single payroll structure, he ordered that it be done."

"And did the Canal Zone government comply?"

"No. That is, Governor Newcomer resorted to subterfuge. He made it look like he was complying by removing the gold and silver labels and replacing them with "U.S. rate" and "local rate" and even made a single pay scale by tacking on the "silver" pay scale at the bottom of the "gold" pay scale, end to end, to give the semblance of a single wage ladder, thus keeping the status quo." (What a trickster!)

Here panelist #2 jumped in.

"And to show how mean they could be, when the law was passed requiring equal pay for equal work that would cover Panamanian West Indians who were doing skilled work for low wages and on the canal zone they were required to comply, the MTC/CLU put a wrinkle into that baby by saying, yes, but they would have to complete an apprenticeship program or a qualified OJT program first, knowing full well that that would eliminate all local rate employees because only U.S. citizens had access to apprenticeship programs. Every time changes were ordered that would end some form of discrimination, the local white power structure found a way to resist or circumvent the orders."

"Then how were they ever going to get these people to change anything if even the President couldn't get them to change?"

"On that score," said panelist #3, "give Harry Truman some credit; he was no fool and he was just as determined as they were. Because of their stubbornness he had the General Accounting Office audit the Canal Company's books and as a result of their findings which confirmed all previous reports, in 1950 he removed the Canal Zone funding from an appropriation status[31] so they wouldn't receive budget allocations directly from Congress (a political body), and ordered that the Canal Zone government operate entirely from the revenues collected as tolls in the Canal. This meant that they had to go through the Federal Government Accounting Office (GAO), and not the political patronage of congress. Every penny would have to be accounted for and there would be no more "padding" of budget requests, no more "cronyism", no more "hidden fat" in the budget, big paychecks and a lot of "goodies" heretofore enjoyed such as 50% tropical differential on top of their fat salaries, hefty raises and hefty vacation packages for both spouses, free rent, two weeks sick leave per year, two months' cumulative vacation with pay, free round-trips to the United States twice a year for the entire family, etc."

"In that way he was punishing the white people who were resisting him, but how did that help the West Indians who were suffering?" asked someone in the audience.

Panelist #3 responded.

"That's a good question because in a way it didn't help them at all since the Zonians in retaliation would take it out on the West Indians by passing on the cuts and increased costs to West Indians in every devious way that they could. Also in 1950 they had Local 713 branded as a communist organization which had to be disbanded and even when it was reorganized under the new name, Local 900, and President Gaskin presented to Governor Francis Newcomer a set of union demands for equality[32] for local rate employees including the following:

- A true single wage scale

- U.S. minimum wages

- Equal pay for equal work

- Elimination of race or national origin as qualification for certain positions

- Elimination of racial segregation

- Automatic step increases in grade (as with U.S.-rate employees)

- Differential pay for night work

- Seniority rules for reductions-in-force and rehiring

- Regular grievance procedures to protect against overbearing supervisors

- Increase in disability relief with a minimum of $60/mo.

- Six months notification of permanent retirement

- More and better housing

- Separate sick leave and vacation

- Payment by check

- Elimination of racial segregation/discrimination

- Quarters for retirees pending repatriation

- Free outpatient medical care for dependents

Governor Newcomer used the Truman reorganization plan itself as an excuse not to be able to find the funds to meet any of these demands, claiming that there were no more appropriations and no way to pay for them.

But it got worse. In 1953 and 1954 politics got very heated when the Panamanian government joined forces with the West Indian labor union in the Canal Zone in seeking a new treaty with the U.S. favorable to Panama. There were rallies and meetings, denunciations of the C. Z. government, big open air crowds with grand speeches and there were many promises made by Panama's President Jose Antonio Remon to Ed Gaskin and the W. I. workers in return for the backing of local 900 Labor Union that gave to Remon their complete support expecting great benefits in return for West Indian workers in the Canal Zone after the treaty was signed. But, as it turned out, Remon sold out the West Indians[33] when he secretly agreed to terms in the treaty that were favorable only to nationalist Panamanians and to the Panamanian business sector but nothing for the West Indians who paid the following price instead:

- Local rate Panamanian West Indian employees' wages on the canal zone became subjected to Panama's income taxes.

- Panamanians who lived outside the Canal Zone lost commissary privileges (the right to shop in the canal zone which means they would have to shop in Panama).

- Hundreds of local rate employees lost their jobs due to transfer of certain operations from the zone government to Panama.

- Depopulation of West Indians from the canal zone forced them into Panama to live and to be exploited by Panamanian businessmen.

- West Indian employees gained nothing from this treaty.

Governor John Seybold, anticipating the inevitable, seized the opportunity as the perfect excuse he had always wanted in order to justify his evil machinations. First, with regards to President Truman's reorganization plan for cutting costs by penalizing the white privileged class who were gouging the system and refusing to end discriminatory practices on the Canal Zone, one of the ways Seybold gleefully met the cost cuts was by converting all colored schools on the Canal Zone to Latin American schools. He closed the La Boca Jr. College and dismantled and closed down all vocational high school programs such as Wood and Metal Fabrication, Motor Service, Printing Photography, Needlecraft, Business and Homemaking, claiming that by converting all Canal Zone colored schools to Latin American schools with curriculum and language that resembled education provided in Panamanian schools would assimilate Panamanian students into Panama rather than into American society, thus justifying all vocational equipment cost cuts by claiming that in the Spanish high schools they only teach academic subjects and don't need expensive equipment (goodbye technical and vocational training and goodbye vocational high schools).

Also by converting the schools to Latin American schools and eventually turning the schools over to Panama it would end the danger of black and white integration in C. Z. schools and reduce the cost of educating West Indians; but he recklessly ended up dashing the colored schools into chaos and destroying the work that Lawrence Johnson and West Indian educators had accomplished from 1931-1953 in improving the Canal Zone colored schools along U. S. education models. Lawrence Johnson was so devastated by Seybold's actions that in 1953 he tried to resign. He took sick leave and returned to the U. S. where in June, 1953 he had a heart attack and died (some say it was brought on by Seybold's conversions).

With the U. S. Supreme Court's 1954 decision in the Brown vs Board of Education Case that brought about integration in all U. S. schools by law and made white segregationists on the Canal Zone more desperate than ever, Governor Seybold could not wait, not even for a decent conversion plan to fulfill its course over a reasonable period of time; he rushed the conversion immediately (1953-1955) from English to Spanish, without any consideration for the effect it would have on the children who were affected, and for only one reason: to prevent integration.

Governor Seybold's actions, therefore, from his racist point of view, killed three birds with one stone for local white segregationists -- (a) he satisfied Panamanian nationalists' greedy demands at the expense of West Indians; (b) he satisfied Truman's budget cutting reorganization plan at the expense of West Indians; and (c) he avoided integration in the Canal Zone schools that he knew was coming, at the expense of West Indians. But these were not the only deeds in his bag of dastardly tricks -- depopulation of the Canal Zone was the final straw and it went into full effect immediately after the '55 treaty that proved to be a bane to West Indians in the Canal Zone, though many nationalist Panamanians greeted it as a most welcomed gift.

At this point there was a question, or a comment, offered by someone in the audience.

"Would you say that the West Indians made a big mistake in joining with and trusting Remon and the Panamanian government? It's almost as if Remon and his cohorts didn't give a damn about West Indians, in

fact he used them as pawns and scapegoats to bargain with the U.S. and didn't fight for West Indian demands, nor treat them as equals or legitimate Panamanians. Please comment on this."

"Although Remon didn't live to see the full implementation (West Indian sellout) of his 1955 treaty with the U.S., since he was assassinated in January, 1955, sometimes I want to agree with you," responded panelist #3, "since it appears that that bias always was and is and continues to be a problem in Panamanian society and politics. You only have to listen to the things they are saying every day and what they are writing in their tabloids about West Indians (calling them such names as chombos, mecos, anglo-Panamanians, melanoanglos, Africanos etc.) But we could get into an endless debate on that subject going back to the time when the first West Indians arrived in Panama. Some people might even say that the racial prejudices and biases possessed and demonstrated by the Americans against West Indians were acquired and adopted by the native Panamanians; some might say that it was pent up bitterness that stemmed from Panamanian jealousy of West Indians who seemed to the natives to be superior and better off than they were when they first arrived on the Isthmus; some may say it's a culture thing, a desire to identify with a particular way of life and customs, set of values (theirs), as opposed to others, and if you don't sacrifice your own identity and culture and change over to theirs then you are unfit to join their society. The 1941 Panamanian constitution under President Arnulfo Arias Madrid didn't do anything to help that situation in any way and his successor, Ricardo Adolfo De la Guardia was even worse - He told the U.S. he didn't want any more blacks in his country and wanted to get rid of all West Indians. Whatever the answer may be, this question deserves to be treated in a lecture by itself."

"In any case," said panelist #2, "the 1955 treaty did not help the West Indian workers even though Panama was forced eventually to acknowledge first and subsequent generations of West Indians born in Panama as Panamanian citizens; the Panamanian authorities wanted to reduce them to Panama's labor standards and wages rather than elevate them to U.S. standards. Fortunately for those West Indian employees like the teachers in the colored schools who were encouraged by Superintendent Lawrence Johnson to upgrade their education abroad, those who did he promoted to U. S. pay scales and eventually many who stayed till the end came under the Civil Service Retirement Act and received decent benefits in the end in contrast to the vast number of teachers of prior years."

"After 1955, struggles still continued and things continued to get worse in the Panama Canal Zone for West Indians. The workers union was weakened as a result of the '55 treaty; all local rate schools were suddenly converted to Spanish; local rate employees were losing jobs and benefits due to the treaty; many old timers were being disabled and West Indians were being forced off the Canal Zone (Governor Seybold's depopulation plan). The prospect of taking inferior jobs and pay; the prospect of living in inferior housing in Panama (La Boca Town in Rio Abajo is an example), and of being disliked by the Panamanians turned most West Indians off. Fortunately, through the Panama Canal Act of 1979, under the early retirement provision clause, West Indian employees gained special U.S. immigration rights without any waiting period or restriction. This, added to previous U.S. Panamanian treaty agreement, drove the mass migration in the 50's, 60's and 70's from Panama to the United States.

"There were still a number of West Indian workers who remained on the Zone, although the union became smaller and was even further splintered into two more unions to represent workers, local 900 representing Canal Zone civilian personnel, and local 907 representing U.S. army civilian personnel, giving the governor the upper hand (in terms of smaller sized unions. Nevertheless the struggles still continued to go back and forth both with the West Indians struggling against the U.S. Canal Zone Government and also competing against native Panamanians who were now coming for their jobs. What was becoming clear was that after the 1960's West Indian presence and status on the Canal Zone had declined, most old timers had left, died, or were disabled, and those West Indians who remained in Panama were being assimilated into the Spanish culture. West Indian institutions in Panama like the Tribune, the English language sections of daily newspapers, West Indian lodges and societies, associations, businesses and everything associated with West Indian identity were disappearing or being eliminated -- due largely to the Panamanian government's policies and anti-West Indian prejudices.

Meanwhile, as the native Panamanians tasted their new gains, positions, and power through the new treaty, there was more activity on the Panamanian side, for a new generation of militant Panamanian youth in the Institute, spurred by a spirit of nationalism, began to question and challenge the U.S. right to even occupy and govern in any sovereign Panamanian lands. More and more the issue was raised until the question of whose flag should fly over the land and whose laws and police force should secure it, arose.

The first flag incident[34] in 1959 was relatively peaceful. They had made their point and a compromise was worked out but did not indefinitely resolve the issue, since on both sides there was still some disagreement as to Canal Zone sovereignty. In January, 1964, however, in retaliation to American students hoisting the American flag on their campus, hundreds of Panamanian students from the National Institute marched from Panama to Balboa High School[35] campus and attempted to hoist instead the Panamanian flag unto the flagpole as a sign of Panamanian sovereignty. After 3 days of rioting, 21 Panamanians and 3 Americans were dead. And this was the incident that signaled the beginning of the end of U. S. Canal Zone Authority. This, in fact, led 13 years later to the final canal treaty, the U.S.-Panamna treaty of 1977 signed by President Jimmy Carter and General Omar Torrijos that ceded the Panama Canal and the Canal Zone permanently over to Panama."

"What effect did this treaty have on both sides after the signing?" someone in the audience asked.

"Of course there were celebrations on the Panama side; but a lot of people in the U. S. weren't so thrilled, especially in the Republican Party. When

Ronald Reagan became U. S. president he definitely was not happy about it, but of course he couldn't change anything then."

"But how did they manage on the Canal Zone afterwards?"

"Of course," said panelist #1, "the transfer couldn't go into effect immediately; there had to be a transition period. First of all, the treaty had to be ratified by both countries first, and that was accomplished in 1978. Then both countries formed a joint Panama Canal Commission to manage the Canal during a transition period.

A Panama Canal Commission[36], consisting of 9 Board of Directors: 5 Americans and 4 Panamanians, was formed to run canal operations until 1999 when the Panamanian government would then take over completely. The Panama Canal Commission replaced the Panama Canal Company and/or the Canal Zone Government, and the Panama Canal Commission was headed by an Administrator who replaced the governor and who after 1990 would be designated as a Panamanian. The PCC reported to, and set policy for, the Administrator."

"When did the commission take over? And what did the Zone look like under its authority?"

"The Commission authority took effect on 10/1/79, thus officially ending U. S. Canal Zone operations on that date. Under the treaty U. S. rate schools were transferred to the Department of Defense and the Latin American schools to Panama.

Of course with the transfer of the canal operations from the U.S. to Panama that meant that the entire workforce and all jobs and positions, except the ones that came under the Dept. of Defense (U.S. rate schools) and the ones that were eliminated, were transferred to Panama as well, which was a great disadvantage to the remaining West Indian employees. Here the unions, Locals 900 and 907, managed to get their members covered by the Panama Canal Act of 1979 under its early retirement provision clause. Those West Indian employees over age 48 could receive benefits after 18 years of service, so that when large blocks of canal positions were taken over by the Panama Canal Authority, several hundred local-rate employees took early retirement rather than transfer to the Panamanian payroll at a lower pay. In addition, the unions won special U. S. immigration right for up to 15,000 employees who resided in the former Canal Zone, with virtually no waiting period or restrictions. Those local-rate employees who did not choose early retirement either transferred to the Panamanian payroll or were terminated. There were very few terminations as a result.”

Then someone raised the question, facetiously, as to why West Indians don't have much to show for the sacrifices they made in Panama? That question almost caused a bitter argument in the meeting.

“That's a question we must all ask ourselves,” said panelist #1, “not only regarding Panama but everywhere we as black people find ourselves. Before we go blaming our West Indian ancestors who labored in Panama we better consider that all African descendants everywhere have this problem. May be the answer is not as simple as we might be so quick to think. But I really believe that we should schedule a night of discussion or a conference on just this topic alone: Why we as black people don't have much to show for the sacrifices we make in every part of the world? Now I don't want to make any one angry; I just want to make us think. I am sure we can come up with some very good answers to that question and I am very serious about that.”

One of the organizers of the meeting announced that because of the late hour they were closing the session for that evening and next week at the same time they will be conducting another examination this time on the topic: “A LOOK AT PANAMA SOCIETY TODAY FROM AN AFRO-PANAMANIAN PERSPECTIVE.”

After thanking the contributors and everyone who attended this evening she invited them to come to next week's session, then she closed the meeting by thanking them again and wishing everyone a safe return to their homes.

James was satisfied he had gotten a wealth of information to digest. He tucked his notes away, said good night to a few people and headed back to Queens. He thought about the meeting and some of the things he learned. He thought about the topic "A Forgotten People" which was a pamphlet by the same name that some Colonites had written in 1943 about the treatment of West Indians on the Canal Zone and he thought, 'How appropriate a topic it is to describe the "Silver people" who came to that land when there was hardly anything there but a jungle, and he thought of those who came after them. People hardly want to talk about them today anywhere, not in Panama, not in the U.S., not even in their own countries in the Caribbean.'

These days James has plenty of time to reminisce about the past and there are certain things that will never go away. For one thing, he cannot help feeling sadness for the city of Colon. That city where true love for him had once blossomed, that once exciting show place, that fun place with its exotic nightclubs and fine restaurants and theatres, its fine stores on

Front Street, its beautiful municipal palace, its monuments, its attractive national parks, its municipal parks where he and Lisa used to sit, its lovely promenades where they strolled hand in hand, and the plaza where the Colon 'bombero' band used to entertain on Sunday evenings are all gone or tarnished, all are faded or are no more. The place is in such ruin and decay as not to be recognizable, and its residents, those who are still there, are in such dire poverty living amidst the ruin and decay. Back in the forties and early fifties, even after the 1940 fire had decimated one-third or more of that city, which was rebuilt somewhat, there was still some pride and excitement. The Colon Arena was there and was always a packed venue; excursions were still bringing masses of people there to attend fights, see baseball games, take in entertainment, to go shopping, and to go dancing in clubs like the Tropical Club. But of course he feels no sadness for the demise of the American Canal Zone and the Zonians, for they were the originators, the authors of all the trials and suffering that West Indians experienced in the Panama Canal Zone.

Today most, if not all, of the people that he knew, his parents Mr. and Mrs. Edwards, his sisters Ivy and Jean, Mr. and Mrs. Peterson, Sephora and her husband, Iona, Marlene and her lady friends, Lucas the comedian and husband of Marlene, Carlton the dock foreman and his wife Beatrice, the Superintendent of Canal Zone Schools Lawrence Johnson, the Supervisor of Colored schools Alfred E. Osborne, the La Boca Normal School and its dedicated faculty, Local 900 and its courageous leader Ed Gaskin, most of Silver City Jr. High and High School teachers and colleagues, Principal Weakley and most of James's co-workers and fellow teachers, even his one-time best friend Harvey Corbin, all of them are gone. And there is no more United States Canal Zone, that entire era of U.S. occupation and exploitation of the "silver people", that era of "silver" and "gold" towns and facilities, of "U.S. rate" and "local rate", of segregation, humiliation, of social barriers and black powerless-ness, that once police state for blacks and Utopia for whites is no more. It seems almost like a fable today, like a terrible mythical tale in some fiction novel, only it was real, recorded in the book of time, and lives in memory.

One thing has emerged from the past and is still flourishing today on the Atlantic side in a 600-acre plus stretch of land near Manzanillo Bay occupying the southeastern region of Colon, the western part of Coco Solo, all of the former France Field and is still expanding. It is that autonomous enterprise called "The Free Zone or more correctly "The Free Trade

Zone." It has sucked up every drop of life, every ounce of tourism and commerce that used to make Colon a thriving business center once and has now left that city a dried out hollow dead-man's zone. Mayor Bazan had warned West Indians long ago of what was coming and many of them had heeded his warning and left before the disaster was complete. But, O, Colon and its heydays where West Indians once had flourished and had a growing middle class and a social structure and a town that rivaled any town where black people live! Now all the glory days and splendor of Colon, all are gone.

Chapter XVII:

A Quest among the Ruins of Time

James never went back to Rainbow City (except maybe once) after being transferred to La Boca Elementary School in 1952, but he visited Colon on several occasions since then. He wanted to see for himself the ruin and decay of the city he once knew and loved. He couldn't believe that the most romantic years of his life were spent there when he had admired that city and had driven through its streets, strolled in its promenades, walked by its seaside, sat in its parks and held hands with the most beautiful angel and kissed her right there on a park bench near the *statue of Columbus. Fortunately, his memory was not tarnished, only* the city.

In the year 2006 he attended a reunion in Panama City at the Marriott Hotel honoring teachers from the past who taught in Silver City and some, though not all, of his former colleagues were there. It was hosted by former students, graduates of the high school who came through Silver City elementary, junior high and high schools. He was happy to see former colleagues and students, of course, but a little flicker in his heart had hoped that somehow, she might be there. He never saw her, but by a stroke of luck he ran into one of her sisters. He was happy to see Delores, but she was busy at the time engaging other guests. They spoke briefly and she was telling him that Lisa was well and had moved to the U.S. only a few years ago to live with her daughter. She was trying to tell him something else about her but never got to finish before they were separated. They were all much older then, of course, in their early seventies, but what if Lisa was single again? Age does not matter. Delores promised to get back to him later in the evening and give him more information, but, somehow, she got caught up in the celebration and he, too, got caught up in the evening's festivities and later could not find her. At least Lisa was still alive and well, he said to himself. He was obsessed, though, with the desire to find her again for his heart craved to see her once more. Somehow, all the years did not matter. It seems that to a heart that cares time does not matter, for even though everything else and every place else may change, inside the heart it locks away its own reality, fixed in time, and once love has taken roots there it never leaves.

There were two occasions over the years when, he could have sworn, he had seen Lisa. The first time was in 1966 when he was a senior in Brooklyn College. He and his older sister, Ivy, had returned to Panama together to bury their father. He had found out where

Charlie Whyte, a once foster brother, lived and went there to tell him that his foster father, Richard Edwards, had died and we had just buried him yesterday in Corozal cemetery. Charlie lived on 7th Street and Melendez Avenue in Colon. He recognized James as he opened the door.

"Hi Charlie, I'm James, Richard Edward's last son."

"Hi Kiddo, I know who you are. You were a little monkey, but I still remember you." And Charlie welcomed him into his home.

He introduced him to his wife, Maria, and a few of his kids who came in and out of the living room while they sat conversing, and Maria reminded them they were not to go too far because dinner would be ready soon.

"Well, step-brother, how is everything with Dick and Marie, your parents, my foster mom and dad? I haven't seen them in a long time. Is everything all right?"

"You know Charlie, my father and mother always talked about you," said James, "how you were a nice kid and like a son to them."

Charlie always had a wide grin on his face whenever he spoke to you, and he always seemed jovial. He liked to drink a lot, though, and he and his wife had about seven or eight children. They were like rabbits.

"Yes," said Charlie, "your parents took me in and cared for me when I was an orphan. I do not know who my real parents are or how I would have survived without your father, Richard, and your mother, Marie who took care of me. They were like parents to me. I owe them so much! Tell me how are they doing, James?"

"Well, that's why I am here, Charlie. Pops is dead. We buried him yesterday. I don't think my mother knew how to reach you or she would have notified you before. I came down with Ivy from New York day before yesterday and I am sorry you didn't know."

And Charlie just sat there quiet for a moment trying to dry the tears in his eyes, while his wife Maria comforted him. After a few moments he spoke to James.

"I am very sorry, James... If I had only known! I would have loved so much to attend. Your old man and your mother were good to me. Give my love to your mother when you get back to Panama City. Please don't forget."

They talked a while about the other members of the Edwards family, James's brothers and sisters,

Charlie knew them all and there were some joyful moments and incidents they shared during those years but there wasn't enough time to relive them all. He told James he must visit him again and he insisted that he leave his mother's address so he can pay them a visit in the near future. James did not stay for dinner with Charlie and Maria, his wife, and his 8 children, because he felt there were too many mouths to feed although he knew that Charlie and Maria would have stretched it somehow. But he made an excuse that he had eaten already and had to catch the train so he could be back in Panama City by 6:30 p.m.

Charlie was a survivor and it seemed like he took every day of his life as a gift to enjoy and so he never showed any sadness or bitterness as James remembers, and nothing overwhelmed him, not even a house full of children to take care of. He was an auto mechanic, and a good one, too, and with that trade he was able to take care of his family.

Anyway, when he left Charlie and he was returning to Panama on the train, in the front of the same car James saw someone that looked like Lisa. His heart leaped and he wanted to do the same in her direction, but she was with someone else who he supposed was her husband. She saw him, too, he thought, for she looked at him and she smiled that same sweet smile that he remembers. His bliss did not last very long, however, as they both got up and disembarked at the next station. There went his love again, he said to himself, before he could even verify that it was she, or speak to her, which he would have done if it didn't happen so fast. It happened too quickly, and they were gone.

The next occasion was in 1985, when he had visited Panama to attend a celebration honoring the diggers of the Panama Canal, and he and some friends drove over to Colon. When they made a stop for one of them to take care of some personal business, he had told them he would be right back. He had had the urge to walk by the second street park which wasn't far from where they stopped, and then he crossed the street and was walking by the statue of "Colon" in the Centenario park on Avenida Central and could have sworn he saw someone looking like Lisa sitting on a park bench with a little girl sitting beside her. At that moment the friends whom he was with drove up in their car and called to him to get in that he had wandered off and they were looking all over for him. He asked them if they could wait just a moment and when he turned to go toward the lady sitting on the park bench she had disappeared. They asked him what was wrong if he had seen a ghost. And he said "No, it was nothing." And they drove off.

August 14, 2013, was one of those very hot days in the summer in Queens, New York City, and it found James at home in Springfield Gardens reminiscing and going through some old memorabilia. Among the publications he was perusing was the journal he had received in 2006 during the Rainbow City High School reunion celebration in Panama City honoring teachers of the past. He had looked cursorily through the journal many times before, but this time he took more care and read through it painstakingly checking every detail, and when he came to the pages with pictures of all high school graduates, there, on one of the pages of the graduating classes, was the love of his life as young and beautiful as he remembered her. He looked at it for almost 10 minutes and every moment of every day he had spent with her came back to him. Memory is such a wonderful gift and a picture is truly worth a thousand words.

But now he must focus all his effort if he is going to achieve the one goal he cannot leave undone in life, and that is, to find Lisa Peterson again. He began by having conversations with old friends from Colon who were still alive and posing questions to them about their recollections of what Colon used to look like, of old neighborhoods and people and places they used to know and what became of them. But in that kind of nostalgia pot luck discussion the name he was interested in he never mentioned though he hoped, by chance, that the other person would. It was like playing the lottery and hoping that your number shows up as the winning number. The odds weren't too great. If he was going to mention the name of the person he was looking for and his motives, he would have to ask someone he knows very well whom he could trust. Very few people he knew fit that requirement to get into his personal business. But he was lucky, two very dear friends, a former classmate, Daryl Anders and his wife Pearlina were from the former Silver City and they knew Lisa and her sisters, and he knew he could trust Pearlina and Daryl. "It's been many years since I saw them and we were not that close," said Pearlina, "but I seem to recall them living in Silver City and Lisa, yes, Lisa suddenly got married to a guy from Almirante named Henry Stewart who had relocated to Silver City. I believe he passed away several years ago. I can make some inquiries for you to see if I can find out anything more about what happened to Lisa."

"Thanks, Pearlina, I appreciate any information you can find out for me. I know you must think I am an old fool for holding onto the past, but I just cannot let it go."

"No, no, James, far from me to think that. Look here, I'll tell you a story and you'll see why. There was this couple I once knew in Silver City who used to date when they were young and in high school in the Canal Zone. They were madly in love with each other but the girl's parents didn't want him for a son-in-law and did everything to stop it until they succeeded in breaking up the relationship with ultimatums and threats. She didn't want to defy her parents or to turn against them and he decided rather than have a nasty fight with them, for her sake he would leave her alone and he went away. You know, some 20 years later I met him here in the United States and he happened to mention her name. I knew the girl; at the time he and I talked, she was living in Queens, N.Y. alone with her son and when I told him that, the man just lit up with so much joy on his face. He said to me that he was trying to find out what became of her for so long but no one could tell him anything until he met me. I never saw anything like that; he would not give me peace unless and until I gave him her address and her telephone number. And right then and there he called her on the phone and the two of them broke down and cried like babies while they were talking over the telephone. I've never seen anything like that and guess what, the most remarkable thing was that he is the father of her son and all these years he never even knew he had a son, and she didn't know where to find him to tell him, because her parents had chased him away. To make a long story short, he took the first plane from Georgia and flew straight to Queens, married that girl and today they are the happiest couple and family you ever met. You see how fate and providence work in people's lives. So that's why I say anything can happen, maybe providence will work in your case too, so keep trying to find your lost love."

"That story has a beautiful ending, thanks for telling me, Pearlina."

And with that they said they would talk again soon, and he asked her to give his regards to her husband who was taking a nap at the time he called but he didn't want her to wake him.

Several months later he still hadn't heard from Pearlina and he hesitated to call her and ask. He knew that if she had any information, she would have called him already and he would not have to ask her for it, so he concluded that she hadn't any additional news to tell him. He was grateful, however, for the fact that she told him Lisa was a widow and was no longer tied to anyone. In the meantime he still continued his search.

In the beginning of the year 2014 he started having dreams about Lisa and about meeting her again. He was affected most by a dream he had of that day long ago, April 19, 1951, when they kissed each other passionately in the park and vowed to always love each other. The anniversary of that day was soon approaching, and he decided it was a good time to return to Panama to visit his only surviving brother who lived in Parque Lefevre, Panama City. He wrote him that he was coming to visit and when he arrived in Panama his brother was overjoyed to see him and they exchanged pleasantries and old stories of their parents, their siblings, and old friends they once knew. After several days passed the 19th of April approached and with it the memory of the past, in the dream he had, was drawing him back to Colon, if only to visit one last time the scene where he and Lisa first sat and exchanged vows of love. He told his brother he had to go there to see an old friend on April 19th and he would be back late that evening or the next day. His brother offered to drive him to the station and suggested that he take the bus to Colon instead, which is cheaper, rather than the train that is very expensive these days. He said, "No, just drop me off by the Corozal railroad station." He decided to pay the exorbitant $25 fare to ride the railroad train to Colon knowing that the bus was a lot cheaper, he didn't care what the cost was anyway. He didn't care how decadent and how ruined and crime-ridden the city of Colon had become, either. He only knew he had to answer the urge that was compelling him to go there that day and nothing else mattered.

So, on the 19th of April they left Parque LeFevre early to catch the 7:15 a.m. train, the only daily train those days going to Colon which arrived at approximately 8:15 a.m. Some of the good things about the new train were that it had a bathroom, was air-conditioned, had wider windows, and they served you a small cup of instant coffee and a cookie, that was all the luxury you got for $25; but of course the ride was also pleasant and the view along the canal route was even spectacular -- balderdash! The trains of prior years had the same view for a cheaper fare ($1.25).

He arrived in Colon at around 8:20 a.m. at a time when most businesses and stores were not yet open and there were only a few early peddlers and street loafers stirring about. Before long there would be a number of street carts and street venders and lottery venders up and down. There were a lot of unemployed and desperate people in Colon so he knew he was taking chances wandering about the town unless he had a safe and a specific address where he was going. As he was leaving the station some strangers who were on the same train approached him. They were impressed by him when they had heard him conversing with another passenger on the train during the trip from Panama.

"Sir, can you give us a few directions, we are complete strangers."

"Sure, I'll be glad to help you, I am a little familiar with Colon," he said to them, "I used to live here many years ago. One piece of advice I can give you, though, you must always be very careful in this town since there's a lot of crime in the streets and you could be easily victimized because people are very desperate."

"Thank you for that advice," they said, "can you tell us where we can safely go, then, to get some decent food in a nice sit-down restaurant; and how we can get transportation to the Free Trade Zone, to Agua Clara Locks and to Gatun Locks and then return to Panama City without taking that expensive railroad train?"

"Well, as far as what to see, you mentioned the Free Zone. It is on the southeast side only about fifteen minutes from here, but that would take a whole day, maybe two to see all there is to see and to shop. If you didn't bring a whole lot of money to spend and have the time then there is no point going there, it's mostly best for wholesale shopping; then there's the Agua Clara Locks, the new 3rd locks built for larger ships but that won't be operational and open for tourists until the beginning of next year; then there's Portobelo National Park along the north shore

10 miles from Colon where the Spaniards used to store and ship their bounty from Panama to Spain; and there is Port Colon 2000 near the east side where we are going with many attractions to see; and there's Manzanillo International Terminal where all the big tourist ships and cargo ships now dock to bring passengers and cargo to the Free Zone. But, as I said, these tours all take a full day mostly and have to be booked in advance. If you plan to stay in Panama for a good length of time you should check these tours out wherever you are staying and book them from there since many of them may require reservations with professional tour guides. This side of Colon used to be a popular tourist stop when Front Street was an attractive tourist site with exotic Indian stores with beautiful Indian furniture, costumes and jewelry. But this area has declined a great deal especially since the Free Zone was built. Where dining is concerned, there are a few restaurants nearby but they only open for lunch and dinner. If you would like to join me I am going to a nice restaurant where they serve breakfast, the food is good and there's a good ocean view where we can sit and can discuss your plans while having something to eat. It is on the east side on Calle Paseo Gorgas overlooking Manzanillo Bay where you will see all the big ships docked.

"That sounds good, what do you suggest we do?"

"Since nearby restaurants are not open this early we could take a cab from here to Drake's restaurant which is located in the Radisson Hotel on the east shore near Manzanillo Bay and I'll be glad to join you if that's okay with you?"

"Yes, let's do that. By the way, since we didn't introduce ourselves properly, my name is Judy and this is my husband Richard and these are my two daughters Janie and Susan. We are from Los Angeles, Ca."

"And my name is James, I was born in La Boca, Canal Zone but I lived here in Colon for a number of years before moving back to Panama City, then many years later I went to live in New York City; but I have returned to Panama practically every year since."

It was about 8:35 a.m. when they hailed a cab to take them to Drake's in the Radisson Hotel. They were pleased when they got there and they discovered that most of the customers were tourists like themselves except that many of them were on group tours from their hotels or from the ships in the harbor. They enjoyed the sights along Manzanillo Bay and were happy they made that choice.

After taking in a brief view of the Bay they were just about starved when they and James entered Drake's in the Radisson and sat down to eat with him as their guest. They were so relaxed and contented that they chat for a good while enjoying themselves like they were old friends from a way back until the time caught up with them and they were ready to leave. They had gotten a wealth of information from him that they were sure they would need. They decided to go to the Free Trade Zone another day; but when they left there they would go straight to Gatun Locks and return to Panama and do some shopping.

"Now how do we get to Gatun Locks from here?" asked Judy.

"From here," said James, "you take a cab for the same $3 each going west on Thirteenth Street to the bus terminal not far from the train station where you came from and a bus will take you from there to Gatun Locks. That's a nice tourist site to visit with a sightseeing tour on site, a theatre and tour guide, and a small shopping center. They show a good movie on the history and operation of the locks which you will enjoy. After that I recommend you take another bus from there to go back to Panama City instead of waiting until 5:30 p.m. for the only train and spending another $25 each for a one-way fare. Albrook Field Shopping Mall is a nice place you can visit when you get back to Panama. It is where all the busses stop on their return to Panama City and where most Panamanians go to shop."

They thanked James very much and took a cab to the bus terminal from where they grabbed a bus to Gatun Locks, very happy that they had run into him that morning. This was around 12:45 p.m. when they took off in the cab near the restaurant and James waved at them as they left.

James wasn't going to Colon to visit a friend as he had told his brother; he was going there to rendezvous with a dream from the past and a hope for a miracle that he could not let go. So, when the friends he met on the train departed he decided to walk from the Radisson Hotel to Central Avenue and go north toward 2nd Street to Parque Centenario, although it was quite a good walk but he had plenty of time, so he didn't mind.

When he arrived at the park at about 1:45 p.m., it was warm and sunny. Of course, the park had been modernized a bit but looked mostly the same. There were the familiar-looking park benches, some partly sheltered by the shade of a few trees that blocked out the sunlight. Although slightly different due to aging and remodeling, it was the same place where he and Lisa had sat some 62 years ago and vowed to love each other forever. His thoughts were full of Lisa. Perhaps she, too, had come there many times through the years since April 19, 1951, as he is doing now. What he wouldn't give just to see her again! If only a second miracle could occur! If only as he thought about her, he could see her sitting there, just waiting for him to join her on their favorite park bench! If only as he thought about her, she could appear! He knew those odds were long and near impossible. He knew that when he came to Colon chasing after his dream, and yet, against all odds, he came anyway. The miracle of meeting there today by chance could only happen in his dreams. How strange are chance and fate, and miracles! How strange their unseen hands! As he was about to sit on a familiar park bench that beckoned to him, there was a rose, a beautiful red rose lying on the bench where he was about to sit. It was lying there as yet un-withered, so frail a thing! He picked it up, held it in his hands, and as he sat he thought, 'If this rose could only speak, it could tell him how it got here, for there are no rose bushes growing here!

"O blessed flower," he said, "your loveliness by Time's awesome power shall soon be faded into a memory. Tell me, how came you to be lying here? Could some fair lady, my love perhaps, have placed you here for me to find? For I recall in younger days I placed a rose like you, still fresh and glowing, still sweet with the breath of spring, into a lock of my love's hair. Tell me, was she the one who placed you here, not long ago before I came? Your beauty has not yet felt the blight, nor cruelty of Time's unpitying power that changes everything." This must be a miracle then, he thought to himself. Why not? It looks Just like the rose she once wore in her hair for him.

"O tell me this was not by chance, but it was Lisa, herself, who left you here for me to find. Miracles happen often in many strange ways. For this rose, then, I give thee, angels, thanks for making my trip today not all in vain."

And, so, believing he had found something of hers that he could hold, that his heart could cling to, gave to him immeasurable joy! He sat there on the park bench, all alone, for a good while speculating, contemplating, remembering the past, and then he arose, the priceless little treasure in his hand, and left the park.

A few days later he departed from Panama and he never returned to Colon again. He and Lisa have never seen each other again and the chances that they will grow slimmer and slimmer as the window of time closes and the past becomes a distant memory. It may be, though, that one day in some place where miracles happen two or three times, two lovers from the past with hope still in their hearts will find, at last, their final miracle.

FOOTNOTES:

CHAPTER I

1. FDR travels, visit to Balboa, C.Z. 7-12-34, National Archives

2. PWIHA journal: Torchbearers to Glory 1925-1955, publ. by PWIHA 1987

CHAPTER II

3. Silver and gold rates and benefits, page 39, 40, 41: "Los Inmigrantes Antillanos en Panama by George Westerman, cc 1980

4. Black Labor on a White Canal by Michael Conniff, p. 50, par 1-6, lines 7+…."…gold roll pay is meant to be substantially greater and gold roll benefits include spaciously furnished free housing, sick leave, and paid home leave, plus overseas differential, etc.. It is the policy of the Commission to keep employees who are undoubtedly black or belong to mixed races on the Silver Roll. Only Americans are to be on the gold roll.

CHAPTER III

5. A.L.B. Morgan, p. 19 ..."Pioneers in Canal Zone Education" by George Westerman, publ. in 1949 for Negro History Week by the La Boca Occupational High School Press.

CHAPTER IV

6. Pearl Harbor and the Birth of the Civil Rights Movement written by Thomas W. Cutrer and T. Michael Parrish, cc 2017 pub Texas A & M Press.

7. Arnulfo Arias' 1941 Constitution, pp. 4-8, Articles 12-14, "Afro Panavision.com News Magazine" June, 2015 Issue, Vol. 8, No. 47; Westerman, "Fifty Years," pp. 122-25.

8. Arnulfo Arias, 1941... pp. 99-100 (on page 99, par. 1 famous remark referring to West Indians, "I will not do as the Nazis do. I will not shoot them) "Black Labor on a White Canal 1904-1981," by Michael A. Conniff, University of Pittsburgh Press, 1985.

9. Ricardo Adolfo de la Guardia -- hated West Indians more than Arnulfo Arias. Westerman Interview, 16 April 1981; P.C. Annual Report, 1942, pp. 113-14.

10. National Civic League of Panama....p. 98, par. 5;
    p. 103, par.2, lines 8-15, "Black Labor on a White
    Canal 1904-1981," Michael Conniff, pub. Univ. of
    Pittsburgh Press, 1985.

11. Osborne: RCHS Newsletter, Sept. 2005, vol. 3, no.
    17, p.2, par. 7-10; p.3, par. 1-8.

12. Osborne: RCHS Newsletter, Dec., 2006, vol. 4, no.
    23, p. 2, par. 6 and p.3, par. 1

13. Osborne... "Black Labor on a White Canal" by
    Michal Conniff, p. 92, par. 3, 4; p. 93; p.94, par.
    1, 2; p. 95

14. Disability Relief...$l.00 per year service up to a
    maximum of $25 per month reducible by x amount
    depending on their possessions or bank account, P.
    11, lines10-13, "Blacks Played Significant Role in
    Improving Life in Isthmus of Panama" by Ed.
    Gaskin, 1983.

15. Disability Relief...p. 69, "Los Inmigrantes
    Antillanos en Panama" by George Westerman,
    1980.

16. Panama Tribune, 2 April, 1950, Raymond Allan Davis, "West Indian Workers on the Panama Canal: A Split Labor Market Interpretation," PhD diss., Stanford University, 1981, pp. 169-71.

17. President Enrique A. Jimenez…Library of Congress id, VIAF id

18. Lawrence Johnson…"Black Labor on a White Canal" by Michael Conniff, pp. 120-121.

19. A tribute to Lawrence Johnson (7/4/1901 – 6/5/1953), "In Memoriam" by Joselyn H. Thompson pub. La Boca Jr. College Yearbook, El Pacifico, 1954.

20. Alfred E. Osborne" Afro-Panavision.com/Afro-Panamanian.com, Notable Creole Icons.

21. General Objectives of the Canal Zone Colored Schools: A Curriculum Monograph by Alfred E. Osborne, Leonor Jump, P. S. Martin, mimeographed at Balboa Heights, C. Z., 1938.

22. Unionism, significant role played by Ed. Gaskin –
RCH Newsletter, Sept. 2006, vol. 4, No. 22, pp. 1-
4.

23. Ewart Guinier, b. Panama 1910, immigrated to
Boston, U. S. A. 1925, Harvard grad, became
professor and chairman Afro-American Studies
Dept. in later years. In 1948 he joined forces with
Paul Robeson and W.E.B. DuBois to launch a
Citizens' Committee to End Silver-Gold Jim Crow
in the Panama C. Z.

Article from The Global South: "Race and Politics
in Concert, vol. 6, No. 2, Fall 2013, pp. 107-129,
p. Indiana University Press, auth. Kathleen Zien.

24. "I never have and never will sing in places where
my people are segregated in the
audience"...Robeson. "Race and Politics in
Concert: Paul Robeson & Paul Warfield in Concert
in Panama 1947-1953, by Kathleen Zien, 2013,
Indiana University Press.

25. "Pioneers in Canal Zone Education" by George W.
Westerman, published by La Boca and Silver City
High Schools, printed in La Boca Occupational High
School printing shop, 1949.

CHAPTER XVI

26. Wikipedia – free encyclopedia, History of the Panama Canal

-- The U. S. and the Panama Canal, par. 2-3

27. Rainbow City High Newsletter, vol. 4, September 2006, No. 22,

pp.1, par. 1

28. Rainbow City High Newsletter, vol. 4, No. 19, January 2006

pp. 3, par. 2

29. International Labor Organization Conference, Philadelphia, 1944

30. Rainbow City High Newsletter, vol. 4, No. 19, January 2006,

Par. 2, lines 16-28

31. 1936 Roosevelt--Harmodio Arias Treaty; Cordell Hull—Alfaro

Agreement with Cordell Hull note re equal employment practice between U.S. and Panama on the Canal Zone.

32. Rainbow City High Newsletter, vol. 4, No. 19, January 2006,

pp. 5, par 1

33. Rainbow City High Newsletter, vol. 4, No. 22, September 2006,

pp. 2, par. 4

34. Rainbow City High Newsletter, vol. 4, No. 22, September 2006,

pp. 3

35. Rainbow City High Newsletter, vol. 4, No. 22, September 2006,

pp. 4, par. 2

Major, Prize Possession, pp. 382 - Governor Fleming 2/1/62 - 1/31/67

U.S. National Archives: Panama Canal Riots, Treaties, Elections,

1959 - 1973

36. 1964 riot – publication "1976 Anthrax Strike, Michael Murphy,

IBEW Local Union 520, Senior Seminar, October 2005

Knapp, Red, White & Blue Paradise, pp.54-57.

Michael Conniff, Black Labor on a White Canal, p. 145

U.S. National Archives: Panama Canal Riots, Treaties, Elections, etc., 1959 – 1973

37. Agency, Executive Branch, United States Government provided for by the Panama Canal Treaty of 1977 (11AAS – 10030) and established by the Panama Canal Act of 1979 (Public Law 96 – 70; 22 U.S.C. 3601 et seq) enacted September 27, 1979.